STRANGE
PILGRIMS

STRANGE PILGRIMS

Twelve Stories by
Gabriel García Márquez

TRANSLATED FROM THE SPANISH

BY EDITH GROSSMAN

Alfred A. Knopf   New York   1993

THIS IS A BORZOI BOOK
PUBLISHED BY ALFRED A. KNOPF, INC.

Originally published in Spanish as *Doce cuentos peregrinos*
by Mondadori España, S.A., Madrid.

Some of the stories in this collection were originally published
in the following:
The New Yorker: "*Bon Voyage*, Mr. President" and
"Maria dos Prazeres"
The Paris Review: "The Saint"
Playboy: "Sleeping Beauty and the Airplane,"
"The Happy Summer of Miss Forbes"
(now titled "Miss Forbes's Summer of Happiness"),
and "The Trail of Your Blood in the Snow"

Library of Congress Cataloging-in-Publication Data
García Márquez, Gabriel, [*date*]
[Doce cuentos peregrinos. English]
Strange pilgrims / by Gabriel García Márquez ;
translated by Edith Grossman.
p.   cm.
ISBN 0-679-42566-7
1. Latin Americans—Europe—Fiction. I. Title.
PQ8180.17.A73D6313   1993
863—dc20   93-12257 CIP

Manufactured in the United States of America
First American Edition

Contents

Prologue: Why Twelve, Why Stories, Why Pilgrims

The twelve stories in this book were written over the last eighteen years. Before they reached their current form, five of them had been journalistic notes and screenplays, and one was a television serial. Fifteen years ago I recounted another during a taped interview with a friend who transcribed and published the story, and now I've rewritten it on the basis of his version. This has been a strange creative experience that should be explained, if only so that children who want to be writers when they grow up will know how insatiable and abrasive the writing habit can be.

The first story idea came to me in the early 1970s, the result of an illuminating dream I had after living in Barcelona for five years. I dreamed I was attending my own funeral, walking with a group of friends dressed in solemn mourning but in a festive mood. We all seemed happy to be together. And I more than anyone else, because of the wonderful opportunity that death afforded me to be with my friends from Latin America, my oldest and dearest friends, the ones I had not seen for so long. At the end of the service, when they began to disperse, I attempted to leave too, but one of them made me see with decisive finality that as far as I was concerned, the party was over. "You're the only one who can't go," he said. Only then did I understand that dying means never being with friends again.

I don't know why, but I interpreted that exemplary dream as a conscientious examination of my own identity, and I thought this was a good point of departure for writing about the strange things that happen to Latin Americans in Europe. It was a heartening find, for I had just finished *The Autumn of the Patriarch*, my most difficult and adventurous work, and I did not know where to go from there.

For some two years I made notes on story subjects as they occurred to me, but could not decide what to do with them. Since I did not have a notebook in the house on the night I resolved to begin, my children lent me one of their composition books. And on our frequent travels they were the ones who carried it in their schoolbags for fear it would be lost. I accumulated sixty-four ideas with so many detailed notes that all I needed to do was write them.

In 1974, when I returned to Mexico from Barcelona, it became clear to me that this book should not be the novel it had seemed at first, but a collection of short stories based on journalistic facts that would be redeemed from their mortality by the astute devices of poetry. I already had published three volumes of short stories, yet none of them had been conceived and composed as a whole. On the contrary, each story had been an autonomous, occasional piece. And therefore writing these sixty-four story ideas might be a fascinating adventure if I could write them all in a single stroke, with an internal unity of tone and style that would make them inseparable in the reader's memory.

I composed the first two—"The Trail of Your Blood in the Snow" and "Miss Forbes's Summer of Happiness"—in 1976, and published them soon afterward in various literary supplements in several countries. I continued working without a break, but in the middle of the third story, the one about my funeral, I felt myself tiring more than if I had been working on a novel. The same thing happened with the fourth. In fact, I did not have the energy to finish them. Now I know why: The effort involved in writing a short story is as intense as beginning a novel, where everything must be defined in the first paragraph: structure, tone, style, rhythm, length, and sometimes even the personality of a character. All the rest is the pleasure of writing, the most intimate, solitary pleasure one can imagine, and if the rest of one's life is not spent correcting the novel, it is because the same iron rigor needed to begin the book is required to end it. But a story has no beginning, no end: Either it works or it doesn't. And if it doesn't, my own experience, and the experience of others, shows that most of the time it is better for one's health to start again in another direction, or toss the story in the wastebasket. Someone, I don't remember who, made the point with this comforting phrase: "Good writers are appreciated more for what they tear up than for what they publish." It's true I didn't tear up the first drafts and notes, but I did something worse: I tossed them into oblivion.

I remember having the composition book on my desk in Mexico, shipwrecked in a squall of papers, until 1978. One day, when I was looking for something else, I realized I hadn't seen it for some time. It didn't matter. But when I was sure it really wasn't on the desk, I panicked. Every corner of the house was searched. We moved furniture, pulled the library apart to be certain it hadn't fallen behind the books, and subjected the household help and our friends to unforgivable inquisitions. Not a trace. The only possible—or plausible?—explanation was that in one of my frequent campaigns to exterminate papers, the notebook had gone into the trash.

My own reaction surprised me: The subjects I had forgotten about for almost four years became a question of honor. In an attempt to recover them at any cost, and with labor that was as arduous as writing, I managed to reconstruct the notes for thirty stories. Since the very effort of remembering acted as a purge, I eliminated without pity the ones that seemed beyond salvation and was left with eighteen. This time I was determined to write without a break, but I soon realized I had lost my enthusiasm for them. And yet, contrary to the advice I always give young writers, I did not throw them out. I refiled them instead. Just in case.

When I began *Chronicle of a Death Foretold*, in 1979,

Prologue

I confirmed the fact that in the pauses between books I tended to lose the habit of writing, and it was becoming more and more difficult for me to begin again. That is why, between October 1980 and March 1984, I set myself the task of writing a weekly opinion column for newspapers in various countries, as a kind of discipline for keeping my arm in shape. Then it occurred to me that my struggle with the material in the notebook was still a problem of literary genres and they should really be newspaper pieces, not stories. Except that after publishing five columns based on the notebook, I changed my mind again: They would be better as films. That was how five movies and a television serial were made.

What I never foresaw was that my work in journalism and film would change some of my ideas about those stories, so that now, when I wrote them in their final form, I had to be very careful to separate my own ideas with a tweezers from those suggested to me by directors while I was writing the scripts. In fact, my simultaneous collaboration with five different creators suggested another method for writing the stories: I would begin one when I had free time, drop it when I felt tired or some unexpected project came along, and then begin another. In a little over a year, six of the eighteen subjects had left for the wastebasket, among them the one about my funeral, for I never could make it the wild revel it had been in my dream. The remaining stories, however, seemed ready to begin a long life.

They are the twelve in this book. Last September, after another two years of intermittent work, they were ready for printing. And that would have concluded their endless pilgrimage back and forth to the trash can if I had not been gnawed by a final, eleventh-hour doubt. Since I had described the European cities where the stories take place from memory, and at a distance, I wanted to verify the accuracy of my recollections after twenty years, and I made a fast trip to reacquaint myself with Barcelona, Geneva, Rome, and Paris.

Not one of them had any connection to my memories. Through an astonishing inversion, all of them, like all of present-day Europe, had become strange: True memories seemed like phantoms, while false memories were so convincing that they replaced reality. This meant I could not detect the dividing line between disillusionment and nostalgia. It was the definitive solution. At last I had found what I needed most to complete the book, what only the passing of the years could give: a perspective in time.

When I returned from that fortunate trip I rewrote all the stories from the beginning in eight feverish months, and because of my helpful suspicion that perhaps nothing I had experienced twenty years before in Europe was true, I did not have to ask myself where life ended and imagination began. Then the writing became so fluid that I sometimes felt as if I were writing for the sheer pleasure of telling a story, which may be the human condition that most resembles levitation. Because I worked on all the stories at the same time and felt free to jump back and forth from one to another, I gained a panoramic view that saved me from the weariness of successive beginnings and helped me track down careless redundancies and fatal contradictions. This, I believe, is how I achieved the volume of stories closest to the one I had always wanted to write.

Here it is, ready to be brought to the table after all its wandering from pillar to post, its struggle to survive the perversities of uncertainty. All the stories except the first two were completed at the same time, and each bears the date on which I began it. The order of the stories in this edition is the same they had in the notebook.

I have always thought that each version of a story is better than the one before. How does one know, then, which is the final version? In the same way the cook knows when the soup is ready, this is a trade secret that does not obey the laws of reason but the magic of instinct. However, just in case, I won't reread them, just as I have never reread any of my books for fear I would repent. New readers will know what to do with them. Fortunately, for these strange pilgrims, ending up in the wastebasket will be like the joy of coming home.

Gabriel García Márquez
CARTAGENA DE INDIAS,
APRIL 1992

STRANGE
PILGRIMS

Bon Voyage, Mr. President

H E S A T O N a wooden bench under the yellow
leaves in the deserted park, contemplating the dusty
swans with both his hands resting on the silver handle of
his cane, and thinking about death. On his first visit to
Geneva the lake had been calm and clear, and there were
tame gulls that would eat out of one's hand, and women
for hire who seemed like six-in-the-afternoon phantoms
with organdy ruffles and silk parasols. Now the only possible woman he could see was a flower vendor on the deserted pier. It was difficult for him to believe that time
could cause so much ruin not only in his life but in the
world.

He was one more incognito in the city of illustrious
incognitos. He wore the dark blue pin-striped suit, brocade vest, and stiff hat of a retired magistrate. He had the

arrogant mustache of a musketeer, abundant blue-black hair with romantic waves, a harpist's hands with the widower's wedding band on his left ring finger, and joyful eyes. Only the weariness of his skin betrayed the state of his health. Even so, at the age of seventy-three, his elegance was still notable. That morning, however, he felt beyond the reach of all vanity. The years of glory and power had been left behind forever, and now only the years of his death remained.

He had returned to Geneva after two world wars, in search of a definitive answer to a pain that the doctors in Martinique could not identify. He had planned on staying no more than two weeks but had spent almost six in exhausting examinations and inconclusive results, and the end was not yet in sight. They looked for the pain in his liver, his kidneys, his pancreas, his prostate, wherever it was not. Until that bitter Thursday, when he had made an appointment for nine in the morning at the neurology department with the least well-known of the many physicians who had seen him.

The office resembled a monk's cell, and the doctor was small and solemn and wore a cast on the broken thumb of his right hand. When the light was turned off, the illuminated X ray of a spinal column appeared on a screen, but he did not recognize it as his own until the doctor used a pointer to indicate the juncture of two vertebrae below his waist.

"Your pain is here," he said.

For him it was not so simple. His pain was improbable and devious, and sometimes seemed to be in his ribs on the right side and sometimes in his lower abdomen, and often it caught him off guard with a sudden stab in the groin. The doctor listened to him without moving, the pointer motionless on the screen. "That is why it eluded us for so long," he said. "But now we know it is here." Then he placed his forefinger on his own temple and stated with precision:

"Although in strictest terms, Mr. President, all pain is here."

His clinical style was so dramatic that the final verdict seemed merciful: The President had to submit to a dangerous and inescapable operation. He asked about the margin of risk, and the old physician enveloped him in an indeterminate light.

"We could not say with certainty," he answered.

Until a short while before, he explained, the risk of fatal accidents was great, and even more so the danger of different kinds of paralysis of varying degrees. But with the medical advances made during the two wars, such fears were things of the past.

"Don't worry," the doctor concluded. "Put your affairs in order and then get in touch with us. But don't forget, the sooner the better."

It was not a good morning for digesting that piece of bad news, least of all outdoors. He had left the hotel very early, without an overcoat because he saw a brilliant sun through the window, and had walked with measured steps from the Chemin du Beau-Soleil, where the hospital was located, to that refuge for furtive lovers, the Jardin Anglais. He had been there for more than an hour, thinking of nothing but death, when autumn began. The lake became as rough as an angry sea, and an outlaw wind frightened the gulls and made away with the last leaves. The President stood up and, instead of buying a daisy from the flower vendor, he picked one from the public plantings and put it in his buttonhole. She caught him in the act.

"Those flowers don't belong to God, Monsieur," she said in vexation. "They're city property."

He ignored her and walked away with rapid strides, grasping his cane by the middle of the shaft and twirling it from time to time with a rather libertine air. On the Pont du Mont-Blanc the flags of the Confederation, maddened by the sudden gust of wind, were being lowered with as much speed as possible, and the graceful fountain crowned with foam had been turned off earlier than usual. The President did not recognize his usual café on the pier because they had taken down the green awning over the entrance, and the flower-filled terraces of summer had just been closed. Inside the lights burned in the middle of the day, and the string quartet was playing a piece by Mozart full of foreboding. At the counter the President picked up a newspaper from the pile reserved for customers, hung his hat and cane on the rack, put on his gold-rimmed glasses to read at the most isolated table, and only then became aware that autumn had arrived. He began to read the international page, where from time to time he found a rare news item from the Americas, and he continued reading from back to front until the waitress brought him his daily bottle of Évian water. Following his doctors' orders, he had given up the habit of coffee more than thirty years before, but had said, "If I ever knew for certain that I was going to die, I would drink it again." Perhaps the time had come.

"Bring me a coffee too," he ordered in perfect French. And specified without noticing the double meaning, "Italian style, strong enough to wake the dead."

He drank it without sugar, in slow sips, and then turned the cup upside down on the saucer so that the coffee grounds, after so many years, would have time to write out his destiny. The recaptured taste rescued him for an instant from his gloomy thoughts. A moment later, as if it were part of the same sorcery, he sensed someone looking at him. He turned the page with a casual gesture, then glanced over the top of his glasses and saw the pale, unshaven man in a sports cap and a jacket lined with sheepskin, who looked away at once so their eyes would not meet.

His face was familiar. They had passed each other several times in the hospital lobby, he had seen him on occasion riding a motor scooter on the Promenade du Lac while he was contemplating the swans, but he never felt that he had been recognized. He did not, however, discount the idea that this was one of the many persecution fantasies of exile.

He finished the paper at his leisure, floating on the sumptuous cellos of Brahms, until the pain was stronger than the analgesic of the music. Then he looked at the small gold watch and chain that he carried in his vest pocket and took his two midday tranquilizers with the last swallow of Évian water. Before removing his glasses he deciphered his destiny in the coffee grounds and felt an icy shudder: He saw uncertainty there. At last he paid the bill, left a miser's tip, collected his cane and hat from the rack, and walked out to the street without looking at the man who was looking at him. He moved away with his festive walk, stepping around the beds of flowers devastated by the wind, and thought he was free of the spell. But then he heard steps behind him and came to a halt when he rounded the corner, making a partial turn. The man following him had to stop short to avoid a collision, and his startled eyes looked at him from just a few inches away.

"Señor Presidente," he murmured.

"Tell the people who pay you not to get their hopes up," said the President, without losing his smile or the charm of his voice. "My health is perfect."

"Nobody knows that better than me," said the man, crushed by the weight of dignity that had fallen upon him. "I work at the hospital."

His diction and cadence, and even his timidity, were raw Caribbean.

"Don't tell me you're a doctor," said the President.

"I wish I could, Señor. I'm an ambulance driver."

"I'm sorry," said the President, convinced of his error. "That's a hard job."

"Not as hard as yours, Señor."

He looked straight at him, leaned on his cane with both hands, and asked with real interest:

"Where are you from?"

"The Caribbean."

"I already knew that," said the President. "But which country?"

"The same as you, Señor," the man said, and offered his hand. "My name is Homero Rey."

The President interrupted him in astonishment, not letting go of his hand.

"Damn," he said. "What a fine name!"

Homero relaxed.

"It gets better," he said. "Homero Rey de la Casa—I'm Homer King of His House."

A wintry knife-thrust caught them unprotected in the middle of the street. The President shivered down to his bones and knew that without an overcoat he could not walk the two blocks to the cheap restaurant where he usually ate.

"Have you had lunch?" he asked.

"I never have lunch," said Homero. "I eat one meal at night in my house."

"Make an exception for today," he said, using all his charm. "Let me take you to lunch."

He led him by the arm to the restaurant across the street, its name in gilt on the awning: Le Boeuf Couronné. The interior was narrow and warm, and there seemed to be no empty tables. Homero Rey, surprised that no one recognized the President, walked to the back to request assistance.

"Is he an acting president?" the owner asked.

"No," said Homero. "Overthrown."

The owner smiled in approval.

"For them," he said, "I always have a special table."

He led them to an isolated table in the rear of the room, where they could talk as much as they liked. The President thanked him.

9

"Not everyone recognizes as you do the dignity of exile," he said.

The specialty of the house was charcoal-broiled ribs of beef. The President and his guest glanced around and saw the great roasted slabs edged in tender fat on the other tables. "It's magnificent meat," murmured the President. "But I'm not allowed to eat it." He looked at Homero with a roguish eye and changed his tone.

"In fact, I'm not allowed to eat anything."

"You're not allowed to have coffee either," said Homero, "but you drink it anyway."

"You found that out?" said the President. "But today was just an exception on an exceptional day."

Coffee was not the only exception he made that day. He also ordered charcoal-broiled ribs of beef and a fresh vegetable salad with a simple splash of olive oil for dressing. His guest ordered the same, and half a carafe of red wine.

While they were waiting for the meat, Homero took a wallet with no money and many papers out of his jacket pocket, and showed a faded photograph to the President, who recognized himself in shirtsleeves, a few pounds lighter and with intense black hair and mustache, surrounded by a crowd of young men standing on tiptoe to be seen. In a single glance he recognized the place, he recognized the emblems of an abominable election campaign, he recognized the wretched date. "It's shocking!" he murmured. "I've always said one ages faster in photographs than in real life." And he returned the picture with a gesture of finality.

"I remember it very well," he said. "It was thousands of years ago, in the cockpit at San Cristóbal de las Casas."

"That's my town," said Homero, and he pointed to himself in the group. "This is me."

The President recognized him.

"You were a baby!"

"Almost," said Homero. "I was with you for the whole southern campaign as a leader of the university brigades."

The President anticipated his reproach.

"I, of course, did not even notice you," he said.

"Not at all, you were very nice," said Homero. "But there were so many of us there's no way you could remember."

"And afterward?"

"You know that better than anybody," said Homero. "After the military coup, the miracle is that we're both here, ready to eat half a cow. Not many were as lucky."

Just then their food was brought to the table. The President tied his napkin around his neck, like an infant's bib, and was aware of his guest's silent surprise. "If I didn't do this I'd ruin a tie at every meal," he said. Before he began, he tasted the meat for seasoning, approved with a satisfied gesture, and returned to his subject.

"What I can't understand," he said, "is why you didn't approach me earlier, instead of tracking me like a bloodhound."

Homero said that he had recognized him from the time he saw him go into the hospital through a door reserved for very special cases. It was in the middle of summer, and he was wearing a three-piece linen suit from the

Antilles, with black and white shoes, a daisy in his lapel, and his beautiful hair blowing in the wind. Homero learned that he was alone in Geneva, with no one to help him, for the President knew by heart the city where he had completed his law studies. The hospital administration, at his request, took the internal measures necessary to guarantee his absolute incognito. That very night Homero and his wife agreed to communicate with him. And yet for five weeks he had followed him, waiting for a propitious moment, and perhaps would not have been capable of speaking if the President had not confronted him.

"I'm glad I did, although the truth is, it doesn't bother me at all to be alone."

"It's not right."

"Why?" asked the President with sincerity. "The greatest victory of my life has been having everyone forget me."

"We remember you more than you imagine," said Homero, not hiding his emotion. "It's a joy to see you like this, young and healthy."

"And yet," he said without melodrama, "everything indicates that I'll die very soon."

"Your chances of recovery are very good," said Homero.

The President gave a start of surprise but did not lose his sense of humor.

"Damn!" he exclaimed. "Has medical confidentiality been abolished in beautiful Switzerland?"

"There are no secrets for an ambulance driver in any hospital anywhere in the world," said Homero.

"Well, what I know I found out just two hours ago from the lips of the only man who could have known it."

"In any case, you will not have died in vain," said Homero. "Someone will restore you to your rightful place as a great example of honor."

The President feigned a comic astonishment.

"Thank you for warning me," he said.

He ate as he did everything: without haste and with great care. As he did so he looked Homero straight in the eye, and the younger man had the impression he could see what the older man was thinking. After a long conversation filled with nostalgic evocations, the President's smile turned mischievous.

"I had decided not to worry about my corpse," he said, "but now I see that I must take precautions worthy of a detective novel to keep it hidden."

"It won't do any good," Homero joked in turn. "In the hospital no mystery lasts longer than an hour."

When they had finished their coffee, the President read the bottom of his cup, and again he shuddered: The message was the same. Still, his expression did not change. He paid the bill in cash but first checked the total several times, counted his money several times with excessive care, and left a tip that merited no more than a grunt from the waiter.

"It has been a pleasure," he concluded as he took his leave of Homero. "I haven't set a date yet for the surgery, and I haven't even decided if I'm going to have it done or not. But if all goes well, we'll see each other again."

"And why not before?" said Homero. "Lázara, my

wife, does cooking for rich people. Nobody makes shrimp and rice better than she does, and we'd like to invite you to our house some night soon."

"I'm not allowed to have shellfish, but I'll be happy to eat it," he said. "Just tell me when."

"Thursday is my day off," said Homero.

"Perfect," said the President. "Thursday at seven I'll be at your house. It will be a pleasure."

"I'll come by for you," said Homero. "Hôtellerie Dames, Fourteen Rue de l'Industrie. Behind the station. Is that right?"

"That's right," said the President, and he stood up, more charming than ever. "It appears you even know my shoe size."

"Of course, Señor," said Homero with amusement. "Size forty-one."

WHAT Homero Rey did not tell the President, but did tell for years afterward to anyone willing to listen, was that his original intention was not so innocent. Like other ambulance drivers, he had made certain arrangements with funeral parlors and insurance companies to sell their services inside the hospital, above all to foreign patients of limited means. The profits were small and had to be shared with other employees who passed around the confidential files of patients with serious illnesses. But it was some consolation for an exile with no future who just managed to support his wife and two children on a ridiculous salary.

Lázara Davis, his wife, was more realistic. A slender mulatta from San Juan, Puerto Rico, she was small and solid, the color of cooked caramel, and had the eyes of a vixen, which matched her temperament very well. They had met in the charity ward of the hospital, where she worked as a general aide after a financier from her country, who had brought her to Geneva as a nursemaid, left her adrift in the city. She and Homero had been married in a Catholic ceremony, although she was a Yoruban princess, and they lived in a two-bedroom apartment on the eighth floor of a building that had no elevator and was occupied by African émigrés. Their daughter, Bárbara, was nine years old, and their son, Lázaro, who was seven, showed signs of slight mental retardation.

Lázara Davis was intelligent and evil-tempered, but she had a tender heart. She considered herself a pure Taurus and believed with blind faith in her astral portents. Yet she had never been able to realize her dream of earning a living as an astrologer to millionaires. On the other hand, she made occasional and sometimes significant contributions to the family's finances by preparing dinners for wealthy matrons who impressed their guests by making them believe they had cooked the exciting Antillean dishes themselves. Homero's timidity was painful, and he had no ambitions beyond the little he earned, but Lázara could not conceive of life without him because of the innocence of his heart and the caliber of his member. Things had gone well for them, but each year was more difficult and the children were growing. At the time of the President's arrival they had begun dipping into their savings of five years. And so when Homero Rey discovered him among the incognito patients in the hospital, their hopes were raised.

They did not know with precision what they were going to ask for, or with what right. At first they planned to sell him the complete funeral, including embalming and repatriation. But little by little they realized that his death did not seem quite as imminent as it had at the beginning. On the day of the lunch they were confused by doubts.

The truth is that Homero had not been a leader of the university brigades or of anything else, and the only part he ever played in the election campaign was to be included in the photograph that they managed to find as if by miracle under a pile of papers in the closet. But his fervor was true. It was also true that he had been obliged to flee the country because of his participation in street protests against the military coup, although his only reason for still living in Geneva after so many years was his poverty of spirit. And so one lie more or less should not have been an obstacle to gaining the President's favor.

The first surprise for both of them was that the illustrious exile lived in a fourth-class hotel in the sad district of Les Grottes, among Asian émigrés and ladies of the night, and ate alone in cheap restaurants, when Geneva was filled with suitable residences for politicians in disgrace. Day after day, Homero had seen him repeat that day's actions. He had accompanied him with his eyes, sometimes at a less than prudent distance, in his nocturnal strolls among the mournful walls and tattered yellow bell-flowers of the old city. He had seen him lost in thought for hours in front of the statue of Calvin. Breathless with the ardent perfume of the jasmines, he had followed him step by step up the stone staircase to contemplate the slow summer twilights from the top of the Bourg-de-Four. One night he saw him in the first rain of the season, without an overcoat or an umbrella, standing in line with the students for a Rubinstein concert. "I don't know why he didn't catch pneumonia," Homero said afterward to his wife. On the previous Saturday, when the weather began to change, he had seen him buy an autumn coat with a fake mink collar, not in the glittering shops along the Rue du Rhône, where fugitive emirs made their purchases, but in the flea market.

"Then there's nothing we can do!" exclaimed Lázara when Homero told her about it. "He's a damn miser who'll give himself a charity funeral and be buried in a pauper's grave. We'll never get anything out of him."

"Maybe he's really poor," said Homero, "after so many years out of work."

"Oh baby, it's one thing to be a Pisces with an ascendant Pisces, and another thing to be a damn fool," said Lázara. "Everybody knows he made off with the country's gold and is the richest exile in Martinique."

Homero, who was ten years her senior, had grown up influenced by news articles to the effect that the President had studied in Geneva and supported himself by working as a construction laborer. Lázara, on the other hand, had been raised among the scandals in the opposition press, which were magnified in the opposition household where she had been a nursemaid from the time she was a girl. As a consequence, on the night Homero came home breathless with jubilation because he had eaten lunch with the President, she was not convinced by the argument that he had taken him to an expensive restaurant. It annoyed her that Homero had not asked for any of the countless things they had dreamed of, from scholarships for the children to a better job at the hospital. The President's decision to leave his body for the vultures instead of spending his francs on a suitable burial and a glorious repatriation seemed to confirm her suspicions. But the final straw was the news Homero saved for last, that he had invited the President for a meal of shrimp and rice on Thursday night.

"That's just what we needed," shouted Lázara, "to have him die here, poisoned by canned shrimp, and have to use the children's savings to bury him."

In the end, what determined her behavior was the weight of her conjugal loyalty. She had to borrow three silver place settings and a crystal salad bowl from one neighbor, an electric coffeepot from another, and an embroidered tablecloth and a china coffee service from a third. She took down the old curtains and put up the new ones, used only on holidays, and removed the covers from the furniture. She spent an entire day scrubbing the floors, shaking out dust, shifting things around, until she achieved just the opposite of what would have benefited them most, which was to move their guest with the respectability of their poverty.

On Thursday night, when he had caught his breath after climbing to the eighth floor, the President appeared at the door with his new old coat and melon-shaped hat from another time, and a single rose for Lázara. She was impressed by his virile good looks and his manners worthy of a prince, but beyond all that she saw what she had expected to see: a false and rapacious man. She thought him impertinent, because she had cooked with the windows open to keep the smell of shrimp from filling the house, and the first thing he did when he entered was to take a deep breath, as if in sudden ecstasy, and exclaim with eyes closed and arms spread wide, "Ah, the smell of our ocean!" She thought him stingier than ever for bringing her just one rose, stolen no doubt from the public gardens. She thought him insolent for the disdain with which he looked at the newspaper clippings of his presidential glories, and the pennants and flags of the campaign, which Homero had pinned with so much candor to the living room wall. She thought him hardhearted, because he did not even greet Bárbara and Lázaro, who had made a gift for him, and in the course of the dinner he referred to two things he could not abide: dogs and children. She hated him. Nevertheless, her Caribbean sense of hospitality overcame her prejudices. She had put on the African gown she wore on special occasions, and her *santería* beads and bracelets, and during the meal she did not make any unnecessary gestures or say a single superfluous word. She was more than irreproachable: She was perfect.

The truth was that shrimp and rice was not one of the accomplishments of her kitchen, but she prepared it with the best will, and it turned out very well. The President took two helpings and showed no restraint in his praise, and he was delighted by the slices of fried ripe plantain and the avocado salad, although he did not share in their nostalgia. Lázara resigned herself to just listening until dessert, when for no apparent reason Homero became trapped in the dead-end street of the existence of God.

"I do believe God exists," said the President, "but has nothing to do with human beings. He's involved in much bigger things."

"I only believe in the stars," said Lázara, and she scrutinized the President's reaction. "What day were you born?"

"The eleventh of March."

"I knew it," said Lázara with a triumphant little start, and asked in a pleasant voice, "Don't you think two Pisces at the same table are too many?"

The men were still discussing God when she went to the kitchen to prepare coffee. She had cleared the table, and longed with all her heart for the evening to end well. On her way back to the living room with the coffee, she was met with a passing remark of the President's, which astounded her.

"Have no doubt, my dear friend: It would be the worst thing that could happen to our poor country if I were president."

Homero saw Lázara in the doorway with the borrowed china cups and coffeepot and thought she was going to faint. The President also took notice. "Don't look at me like that, Señora," he said in an amiable tone. "I'm speaking from the heart." And then, turning to Homero, he concluded:

"It's just as well I'm paying a high price for my foolishness."

Lázara served the coffee and turned off the light above the table because its harsh illumination was not conducive to conversation, and the room was left in intimate shadow. For the first time she became interested in the guest, whose wit could not hide his sadness. Lázara's curiosity increased when he finished his coffee and turned the cup upside down in the saucer so the grounds could settle.

The President told them he had chosen the island of Martinique for his exile because of his friendship with the poet Aimé Césaire, who at that time had just published his *Cahier d'un retour au pays natal*, and had helped him begin a new life. With what remained of his wife's inheritance, the President bought a house made of noble wood in the hills of Fort-de-France, with screens at the windows and a terrace overlooking the sea and filled with primitive flowers, where it was a pleasure to sleep with the sound of crickets and the molasses-and-rum breeze from the sugar mills. There he stayed with his wife, fourteen years older than he and an invalid since the birth of their only child, fortified against fate by his habitual rereading of the Latin classics, in Latin, and by the conviction that this was the final act of his life. For years he had to resist the temptation of all kinds of adventures proposed to him by his defeated partisans.

"But I never opened another letter again," he said. "Never, once I discovered that even the most urgent were less urgent after a week, and that in two months one forgot about them and the person who wrote them."

He looked at Lázara in the semi-darkness when she lit a cigarette, and took it from her with an avid movement of his fingers. After a long drag, he held the smoke in his throat. Startled, Lázara picked up the pack and the box of matches to light another, but he returned the burning cigarette to her. "You smoke with so much pleasure I could not resist," he said. Then he had to release the smoke because he began to cough.

"I gave up the habit many years ago, but it never gave me up altogether," he said. "On occasion it has defeated me. Like now."

The cough jolted him two more times. The pain returned. The President checked his small pocket watch and took his two evening pills. Then he peered into the bottom of his cup: nothing had changed, but this time he did not shudder.

"Some of my old supporters have been presidents after me," he said.

"Sáyago," said Homero.

"Sáyago and others," he said. "All of us usurping an honor we did not deserve with an office we did not know how to fill. Some pursue only power, but most are looking for even less: a job."

Lázara became angry.

"Do you know what they say about you?" she asked.

Homero intervened in alarm:

"They're lies."

"They're lies and they're not lies," said the President with celestial calm. "When it has to do with a president, the worst ignominies may be both true and false at the same time."

He had lived in Martinique all the days of his exile, his only contact with the outside world the few news items in the official paper. He had supported himself teaching classes in Spanish and Latin at an official *lycée*, and with the translations that Aimé Césaire commissioned from time to time. The heat in August was unbearable, and he would stay in the hammock until noon, reading to the hum of the fan in his bedroom. Even at the hottest times of the day his wife tended to the birds she raised in freedom outdoors, protecting herself from the sun with a broad-brimmed straw hat adorned with artificial fruit and organdy flowers. But when the temperature fell, it was good to sit in the cool air on the terrace, he with his eyes fixed on the ocean until it grew dark, and she in her wicker rocking chair, wearing the torn hat, and rings with bright stones on every finger, watching the ships of the world pass by. "That one's bound for Puerto Santo," she would say. "That one almost can't move, it's so loaded down with bananas from Puerto Santo," she would say. For it did not seem possible to her that any ship could pass by that was not from their country. He pretended not to hear, although in the long run she managed to forget better than he because she lost her memory. They would sit this way until the clamorous twilights came to an end and they had to take refuge in the house, defeated by the mosquitoes. During one of those many Augusts, as he was reading the paper on the terrace, the President gave a start of surprise.

"I'll be damned," he said. "I've died in Estoril!"

His wife, adrift in her drowsiness, was horrified by the news. The article consisted of six lines on the fifth page of the newspaper printed just around the corner, in which his occasional translations were published and whose manager came to visit him from time to time. And now it said that he had died in Estoril de Lisboa, the resort and refuge of European decadence, where he had never been and which was, perhaps, the only place

in the world where he would not have wanted to die.
His wife did die, in fact, a year later, tormented by the
last memory left to her: the recollection of her only child,
who had taken part in the overthrow of his father and
was later shot by his own accomplices.

The President sighed. "That's how we are, and nothing can save us," he said. "A continent conceived by the
scum of the earth without a moment of love: the children
of abductions, rapes, violations, infamous dealings, decep-
tions, the union of enemies with enemies." He faced Lázara's African eyes, which scrutinized him without pity,
and tried to win her over with the eloquence of an old
master.

"Mixing the races means mixing tears with spilled
blood. What can one expect from such a potion?"

Lázara fixed him to his place with the silence of death.
But she gained control of herself a little before midnight
and said good-bye to him with a formal kiss. The President refused to allow Homero to accompany him to the
hotel, although he could not stop him from helping him
find a taxi. When Homero came back, his wife was raging
with fury.

"That's one president in the world who really deserved
to be overthrown," she said. "What a son of a bitch."

Despite Homero's efforts to calm her, they spent a terrible, sleepless night. Lázara admitted that he was one of
the best-looking men she had ever seen, with a devastating seductive power and a stud's virility. "Just as he is
now, old and fucked up, he must still be a tiger in bed,"
she said. But she thought he had squandered these gifts of
God in the service of pretense. She could not bear his

boasts that he had been his country's worst president. Or his ascetic airs, when, she was convinced, he owned half the sugar plantations in Martinique. Or the hypocrisy of his contempt for power, when it was obvious he would give anything to return to the presidency long enough to make his enemies bite the dust.

"And all of that," she concluded, "just to have us worshipping at his feet."

"What good would that do him?" asked Homero.

"None at all," she said. "But the fact is that being se-ductive is an addiction that can never be satisfied."

Her rage was so great that Homero could not bear to be with her in bed, and he spent the rest of the night wrapped in a blanket on the sofa in the living room. Lázara also got up in the middle of the night, naked from head to toe—her habitual state when she slept or was at home—and talked to herself in a monologue on only one theme. In a single stroke she erased from human memory all traces of the hateful supper. At daybreak she returned what she had borrowed, replaced the new curtains with the old, and put the furniture back where it belonged so that the house was as poor and decent as it had been until the night before. Then she tore down the press clippings, the portraits, the banners and flags from the abominable campaign, and threw them all in the trash with a final shout.

"You can go to hell!"

A WEEK after the dinner, Homero found the Presi-dent waiting for him as he left the hospital, with the request that he accompany him to his hotel. They climbed three flights of steep stairs to a garret that had a single skylight looking out on an ashen sky; clothes were drying on a line stretched across the room. There was also a double bed that took up half the space, a hard chair, a washstand and a portable bidet, and a poor man's armoire with a clouded mirror. The President noted Homer's reaction.

"This is the burrow I lived in when I was a student," he said as if in apology. "I made the reservation from Fort-de-France."

From a velvet bag he removed and displayed on the bed the last remnants of his wealth: several gold bracelets adorned with a variety of precious stones, a three-strand pearl necklace, and two others of gold and precious stones; three gold chains with saints' medals; a pair of gold and emerald earrings, another of gold and diamonds, and a third of gold and rubies; two reliquaries and a locket; eleven rings with all kinds of precious settings; and a diamond tiara worthy of a queen. From a case he took out three pairs of silver cuff links and two of gold, all with matching tie clips, and a pocket watch plated in white gold. Then he removed his six decorations from a shoe box: two of gold, one of silver, and the rest of no value.

"It's all I have left in life," he said.

He had no alternative but to sell it all to meet his medical expenses, and he asked Homero to please do that for him with the greatest discretion. But Homero did not feel he could oblige if he did not have the proper receipts.

The President explained that they were his wife's jewels, a legacy from a grandmother who had lived in colonial times and had inherited a packet of shares in Colombian gold mines. The watch, the cuff links, and tie clips were his. The decorations, of course, had not belonged to anyone before him.

"I don't believe anybody has receipts for these kinds of things," he said.

Homero was adamant.

"In that case," the President reflected, "there's nothing I can do but take care of it myself."

He began to gather up the jewelry with calculated calm. "I beg you to forgive me, my dear Homero, but there is no poverty worse than that of an impoverished president," he said. "Even surviving seems contemptible." At that moment Homero saw him with his heart and laid down his weapons.

Lázara came home late that night. From the door she saw the jewels glittering on the table under the mercurial light, and it was as if she had seen a scorpion in her bed.

"Don't be an idiot, baby," she said, frightened. "Why are those things here?"

Homero's explanation disturbed her even more. She sat down to examine the pieces, one by one, with all the care of a goldsmith. At a certain point she sighed and said, "They must be worth a fortune." At last she sat looking at Homero and could find no way out of her dilemma.

"Damn it," she said. "How can we know if everything that man says is true?"

"Why shouldn't it be?" said Homero. "I've just seen that he washes his own clothes and dries them on a line in his room, just like we do."

"Because he's cheap," said Lázara.

"Or poor," said Homero.

Lázara examined the jewels again, but now with less attention because she too had been conquered. And so the next morning she put on her best clothes, adorned herself with the pieces that seemed most expensive, wore as many rings as she could on every finger, even her thumb, and all the bracelets that would fit on each arm, and went out to sell them. "Let's see if anyone asks Lázara Davis for receipts," she said as she left, strutting with laughter. She chose just the right jewelry store, one with more pretensions than prestige, where she knew they bought and sold without asking too many questions, and she walked in terrified but with a firm step.

A thin, pale salesman in evening dress made a theatrical bow as he kissed her hand and asked how he could help her. Because of the mirrors and intense lights the interior was brighter than the day, and the entire shop seemed made of diamonds. Lázara, almost without looking at the clerk for fear he would see through the farce, followed him to the rear of the store.

He invited her to sit at one of three Louis XV escritoires that served as individual counters, and over it he spread an immaculate cloth. Then he sat across from Lázara and waited.

"How may I help you?"

She removed the rings, the bracelets, the necklaces, the earrings, everything that she was wearing in plain view,

and began to place them on the escritoire in a chessboard
pattern. All she wanted, she said, was to know their true
value.

The jeweler put a glass up to his left eye and began to
examine the pieces in clinical silence. After a long while,
without interrupting his examination, he asked:

"Where are you from?"

Lázara had not anticipated that question.

"Ay, Señor," she sighed, "very far away."

"I can imagine," he said.

He was silent again, while Lázara's terrible golden eyes
scrutinized him without mercy. The jeweler devoted
special attention to the diamond tiara and set it apart from
the other jewelry. Lázara sighed.

"You are a perfect Virgo," she said.

The jeweler did not interrupt his examination.

"How do you know?"

"From the way you behave," said Lázara.

He made no comment until he had finished, and he ad-
dressed her with the same circumspection he had used at
the beginning.

"Where does all this come from?"

"It's a legacy from my grandmother," said Lázara in
a tense voice. "She died last year in Paramaribo, at the
age of ninety-seven."

The jeweler looked into her eyes. "I'm very sorry," he
said. "But their only value is the weight of the gold." He
picked up the tiara with his fingertips and made it sparkle
under the dazzling light.

"Except for this," he said. "It is very old, Egyptian perhaps, and would be priceless if it were not for the poor

condition of the diamonds. In any case it has a certain historical value."

But the stones in the other treasures, the amethysts, emeralds, rubies, opals—all of them, without exception—were fake. "No doubt the originals were good," said the jeweler as he gathered up the pieces to return them to her. "But they have passed so often from one generation to another that the legitimate stones have been lost along the way and been replaced by bottle glass." Lázara felt a green nausea, took a deep breath, and controlled her panic. The salesman consoled her:

"It often happens, Madame."

"I know," said Lázara, relieved. "That's why I want to get rid of them."

She felt then that she was beyond the farce, and became herself again. With no further delay she took the cuff links, the pocket watch, the tie clips, the decorations of gold and silver, and the rest of the President's personal trinkets out of her handbag and placed them all on the table.

"This too?" asked the jeweler.

"All of it," said Lázara.

She was paid in Swiss francs that were so new she was afraid her fingers would be stained with fresh ink. She accepted the bills without counting them, and the jeweler's leave-taking at the door was as ceremonious as his greeting. As he held the glass door open for her, he stopped her for a moment.

"And one final thing, Madame," he said. "I'm an Aquarius."

Early that evening Homero and Lázara took the money

to the hotel. After further calculations, they found that a little more money was still needed. And so the President began removing and placing on the bed his wedding ring, his watch and chain, and the cuff links and tie clip he was wearing.

Lázara handed back the ring.

"Not this," she said. "A keepsake like this can't be sold."

The President acknowledged what she said and put the ring back on his finger. Lázara also returned the watch and chain. "Not this either," she said. The President did not agree, but she put him in his place.

"Who'd even try to sell a watch in Switzerland?"

"We already did," said the President.

"Yes, but not the watch. We sold the gold."

"This is gold too," said the President.

"Yes," said Lázara. "You may get by without surgery, but you have to know what time it is."

She would not take his gold-rimmed eyeglasses either, although he had another pair with tortoiseshell frames. She hefted the pieces in her hand, and put an end to all his doubts.

"Besides," she said, "this will be enough."

Before she left she took down his damp clothes, without consulting him, to dry and iron them at home. They rode on the motor scooter, Homero driving and Lázara sitting behind him, her arms around his waist. The streetlights had just turned on in the mauve twilight. The wind had blown away the last leaves, and the trees looked like plucked fossils. A tow truck drove along the Rhône, its radio playing at full volume and leaving a stream of music along the streets. Georges Brassens was singing: *Mon amour tiens bien la barre, le temps va passer par là, et le temps est un barbare dans le genre d'Attila; par là où son cheval passe l'amour ne repousse pas.* Homero and Lázara rode in silence, intoxicated by the song and the remembered scent of hyacinth. After a while, she seemed to awaken from a long sleep.

"Damn it," she said.

"What?"

"The poor old man," said Lázara. "What a shitty life!"

ON THE following Friday, the seventh of October, the President underwent five hours of surgery that, for the moment, left matters as obscure as they had been before. In the strictest sense, the only consolation was knowing he was alive. After ten days he was moved to a room with other patients, and Homero and Lázara could visit him. He was another man: disoriented and emaciated, his sparse hair fell out at a touch of the pillow. All that was left of his former presence was the fluid grace of his hands. His first attempt at walking with two orthopedic canes was heartbreaking. Lázara stayed and slept at his bedside to save him the expense of a private nurse. One of the other patients in the room spent the first night screaming with his terror of dying. Those endless nights did away with Lázara's last reservations.

Four months after his arrival in Geneva, he was discharged from the hospital. Homero, a meticulous administrator of the President's scant funds, paid the hospital bill and took him home in his ambulance with other employees who helped carry him to the eighth floor. They put him in the bedroom of the children he never really acknowledged, and little by little he returned to reality. He devoted himself to his rehabilitative exercises with military rigor, and walked again with just his cane. But even in his good clothes from the old days, he was far from being the same man in either appearance or behavior. Fearing the winter that promised to be very severe, and which in fact turned out to be the harshest of the century, he decided, against the advice of his doctors, who wanted to keep him under observation for a while longer, to return home on a ship leaving Marseilles on December 13. At the last minute he did not have enough money for his passage, and without telling her husband Lázara tried to make up the difference with one more scraping from her children's savings, but there too she found less than she expected. Then Homero confessed that without telling her he had used it to finish paying the hospital bill.

"Well," Lázara said in resignation. "Let's say he's our oldest son."

On December 11 they put him on the train to Marseilles in a heavy snowstorm, and it was not until they came home that they found a farewell letter on the children's night table, where he also left his wedding ring for Bárbara, along with his dead wife's wedding band, which he had never tried to sell, and the watch and chain for Lázaro. Since it was a Sunday, some Caribbean neighbors who had learned the secret came to the Cornavin Station with a harp band from Veracruz. The President was gasping for breath in his raffish overcoat and a long multi-

33

colored scarf that had belonged to Lázara, but even so he stood in the open area of the last car and waved good-bye with his hat in the lashing wind. The train was beginning to accelerate when Homero realized he still had his cane. He ran to the end of the platform and threw it hard enough for the President to catch, but it fell under the wheels and was destroyed. It was a moment of horror. The last thing Lázara saw was the President's trembling hand stretching to grasp the cane and never reaching it, and the conductor who managed to grab the snow-covered old man by his scarf and save him in midair. Lázara ran in utter terror to her husband, trying to laugh behind her tears.

"My God," she shouted, "nothing can kill that man."

He arrived home safe and sound, according to his long telegram of thanks. Nothing more was heard from him for over a year. At last they received a six-page hand-written letter in which it was impossible to recognize him. The pain had returned, as intense and punctual as before, but he had resolved to ignore it and live life as it came. The poet Aimé Césaire had given him another cane, with mother-of-pearl inlay, but he had decided not to use it. For six months he had been eating meat and all kinds of shellfish, and could drink up to twenty cups a day of the bitterest coffee. But he had stopped reading the bottom of the cup, because the predictions never came true. On the day he turned seventy-five, he drank a few glasses of exquisite Martinique rum, which agreed with him, and began to smoke again. He did not feel better, of course, but neither did he feel worse. Nevertheless, the real reason for the letter was to tell them that he felt tempted to return to his country as the leader of a reform movement—a just cause for the honor of the nation—even if he gained only the poor glory of not dying of old age in his bed. In that sense, the letter ended, his trip to Geneva had been providential.

JUNE 1979

The Saint

I saw Margarito Duarte after twenty-two years on
one of the narrow secret streets in Trastevere, and at first
I had trouble recognizing him, because he spoke halting
Spanish and had the appearance of an old Roman. His
hair was white and thin, and there was nothing left of the
Andean intellectual's solemn manner and funereal clothes
with which he had first come to Rome, but in the course
of our conversation I began, little by little, to recover him
from the treachery of his years and see him again as he
had been: secretive, unpredictable, and as tenacious as a
stonecutter. Before the second cup of coffee in one of
our bars from the old days, I dared to ask the question
that was gnawing inside me.

"What happened with the Saint?"

"The Saint is there," he answered. "Waiting."

Only the tenor Rafael Ribero Silva and I could understand the enormous human weight of his reply. We knew

his drama so well that for years I thought Margarito Duarte was the character in search of an author that we novelists wait for all our lives, and if I never allowed him to find me it was because the end of his story seemed unimaginable.

He had come to Rome during that radiant spring when Pius XII suffered from an attack of hiccups that neither the good nor the evil arts of physicians and wizards could cure. It was his first time away from Tolima, his village high in the Colombian Andes—a fact that was obvious even in the way he slept. He presented himself one morning at our consulate carrying the polished pine box the shape and size of a cello case, and he explained the surprising reason for his trip to the consul, who then telephoned his countryman, the tenor Rafael Riberto Silva, asking that he find him a room at the *pensione* where we both lived. That is how I met him.

Margarito Duarte had not gone beyond primary school, but his vocation for letters had permitted him a broader education through the impassioned reading of everything in print he could lay his hands on. At the age of eighteen, when he was village clerk, he married a beautiful girl who died not long afterward when she gave birth to their first child, a daughter. Even more beautiful than her mother, she died of an essential fever at the age of seven. But the real story of Margarito Duarte began six months before his arrival in Rome, when the construction of a dam required that the cemetery in his village be moved. Margarito, like all the other residents of the region, disinterred the bones of his dead to carry them to the new cemetery. His wife was dust. But in the grave next to hers, the girl was still intact after eleven years. In fact, when they pried the lid off the coffin, they could smell the scent of the fresh-cut roses with which she had been buried. Most astonishing of all, however, was that her body had no weight.

Hundreds of curiosity-seekers, attracted by the re-sounding news of the miracle, poured into the village. There was no doubt about it: The incorruptibility of the body was an unequivocal sign of sainthood, and even the bishop of the diocese agreed that such a prodigy should be submitted to the judgment of the Vatican. And there-fore they took up a public collection so that Margarito Duarte could travel to Rome to do battle for the cause that no longer was his alone or limited to the narrow con-fines of his village, but had become a national issue.

As he told us his story in the *pensione* in the quiet Parioli district, Margarito Duarte removed the padlock and raised the lid of the beautiful trunk. That was how the tenor Ribero Silva and I participated in the miracle. She did not resemble the kind of withered mummy seen in so many museums of the world, but a little girl dressed as a bride who was still sleeping after a long stay under-ground. Her skin was smooth and warm, and her open eyes were clear and created the unbearable impression that they were looking at us from death. The satin and artificial orange blossoms of her crown had not withstood the rigors of time as well as her skin, but the roses that had been placed in her hands were still alive. And it was in fact true that the weight of the pine case did not change when we removed the body.

Margarito Duarte began his negotiations the day following his arrival, at first with diplomatic assistance that was more compassionate than efficient, and then with every strategy he could think of to circumvent the countless barriers set up by the Vatican. He was always very reserved about the measures he was taking, but we knew they were numerous and to no avail. He communicated with all the religious congregations and humanitarian foundations he could find, and they listened to him with attention but no surprise and promised immediate steps that were never taken. The truth is that it was not the most propitious time. Everything having to do with the Holy See had been postponed until the Pope overcame the attack of hiccuping that proved resistant not only to the most refined techniques of academic medicine, but to every kind of magic remedy sent to him from all over the world.

At last, in the month of July, Pius XII recovered and left for his summer vacation in Castel Gandolfo. Margarito took the Saint to the first weekly audience, hoping he could show her to the Pope, who appeared in the inner courtyard on a balcony so low that Margarito could see his burnished fingernails and smell his lavender scent. He did not circulate among the tourists who came from every nation to see him, as Margarito had anticipated, but repeated the same statement in six languages and concluded with a general blessing.

After so many delays, Margarito decided to take matters into his own hands, and he delivered a letter almost sixty pages long to the Secretariat of State but received no reply. He had foreseen this, for the functionary who accepted his handwritten letter with all due formality did not deign to give more than an official glance at the dead girl, and the clerks passing by looked at her with no interest at all. One of them told him that in the previous year they had received more than eight hundred letters requesting sainthood for intact corpses in various places around the globe. At last Margarito requested that the weightlessness of the body be verified. The functionary verified it but refused to admit it.

"It must be a case of collective suggestion," he said.

In his few free hours, and on the dry Sundays of summer, Margarito remained in his room, devouring any book that seemed relevant to his cause. At the end of each month, on his own initiative, he wrote a detailed calculation of his expenses in a composition book, using the exquisite calligraphy of a senior clerk to provide the contributors from his village with strict and up-to-date accounts. Before the year was out he knew the labyrinths of Rome as if he had been born there, spoke a fluent Italian as laconic as his Andean Spanish, and knew as much as anyone about the process of canonization. But much more time passed before he changed his funereal dress, the vest and magistrate's hat which in the Rome of that time were typical of certain secret societies with unconfessable aims. He went out very early with the case that held the Saint, and sometimes he returned late at night, exhausted and sad but always with a spark of light that filled him with new courage for the next day.

"Saints live in their own time," he would say.

It was my first visit to Rome, where I was studying at the Experimental Film Center, and I lived his calvary with unforgettable intensity. Our *pensione* was in reality a modern apartment a few steps from the Villa Borghese. The owner occupied two rooms and rented the other four to foreign students. We called her Bella Maria, and in the ripeness of her autumn she was good-looking and temperamental and always faithful to the sacred rule that each man is absolute king of his own room. The one who really bore the burden of daily life was her older sister, Aunt Antonietta, an angel without wings who worked for her hour after hour during the day, moving through the apartment with her pail and brush, polishing the marble floor beyond the realm of the possible. It was she who taught us to eat the little songbirds that her husband, Bartolino, caught—a bad habit left over from the war—and who, in the end, took Margarito to live in her house when he could no longer afford Bella Maria's prices.

Nothing was less suited to Margarito's nature than that house without law. Each hour had some surprise in store for us, even the dawn, when we were awakened by the fearsome roar of the lion in the Villa Borghese zoo. The tenor Ribero Silva had earned this privilege: the Romans did not resent his early morning practice sessions. He would get up at six, take his medicinal bath of icy water, arrange his Mephistophelean beard and eyebrows, and only when he was ready, and wearing his tartan bathrobe, Chinese silk scarf, and personal cologne, give himself over, body and soul, to his vocal exercises. He would throw open the window in his room, even when the wintry stars were still in the sky, and warm up with progressive phrasings of great love arias until he was sing-

41

ing at full voice. The daily expectation was that when he
sang his *do* at top volume, the Villa Borghese lion would
answer him with an earth-shaking roar.

"You are the reincarnation of Saint Mark, *figlio
mio*," Aunt Antonietta would exclaim in true amazement. "Only he could talk to lions."

One morning it was not the lion who replied. The
tenor began the love duet from *Otello*—"*Già nella notte
densa s'estingue ogni clamor*"—and from the bottom of
the courtyard we heard the answer, in a beautiful soprano
voice. The tenor continued, and the two voices sang the
complete selection to the delight of all the neighbors, who
opened the windows to sanctify their houses with the
torrent of that irresistible love. The tenor almost fainted
when he learned that his invisible Desdemona was no less
a personage than the great Maria Caniglia.

I have the impression that this episode gave Margarito
Duarte a valid reason for joining in the life of the house.
From that time on he sat with the rest of us at the common table and not, as he had done at first, in the kitchen,
where Aunt Antonietta indulged him almost every day
with her masterly songbird stew. When the meal was
over, Bella Maria would read the daily papers aloud to
teach us Italian phonetics, and comment on the news
with an arbitrariness and wit that brought joy to our
lives. One day, with regard to the Saint, she told us that
in the city of Palermo there was an enormous museum
that held the incorruptible corpses of men, women, and
children, and even several bishops, who had all been disinterred from the same Capuchin cemetery. The news so

disturbed Margarito that he did not have a moment's peace until we went to Palermo. But a passing glance at the oppressive galleries of inglorious mummies was all he needed to make a consolatory judgment.

"These are not the same," he said. "You can tell right away they're dead."

After lunch Rome would succumb to its August stupor. The afternoon sun remained immobile in the middle of the sky, and in the two-o'clock silence one heard nothing but water, which is the natural voice of Rome. But at about seven the windows were thrown open to summon the cool air that began to circulate, and a jubilant crowd took to the streets with no other purpose than to live, in the midst of backfiring motorcycles, the shouts of melon vendors, and love songs among the flowers on the terraces.

The tenor and I did not take a siesta. We would ride on his Vespa, he driving and I sitting behind, and bring ices and chocolates to the little summer whores who fluttered under the centuries-old laurels in the Villa Borghese and watched for sleepless tourists in the bright sun. They were beautiful, poor, and affectionate, like most Italian women in those days, and they dressed in blue organdy, pink poplin, green linen, and protected themselves from the sun with parasols damaged by storms of bullets during the recent war. It was a human pleasure to be with them, because they ignored the rules of their trade and allowed themselves the luxury of losing a good client in order to have coffee and conversation with us in the bar on the corner, or take carriage rides around the paths in the park, or fill us with pity for the deposed monarchs and their tragic mistresses who rode horseback at dusk along the *galoppatoio*. More than once we served as their interpreters with some foreigner gone astray.

They were not the reason we took Margarito Duarte to the Villa Borghese: We wanted him to see the lion. He lived uncaged on a small desert island in the middle of a deep moat, and as soon as he caught sight of us on the far shore he began to roar with an agitation that astonished his keeper. The visitors to the park gathered around in surprise. The tenor tried to identify himself with his full-voiced morning *do*, but the lion paid him no attention. He seemed to roar at all of us without distinction, yet the keeper knew right away that he roared only for Margarito. It was true: Wherever he moved the lion moved, and as soon as he was out of sight the lion stopped roaring. The keeper, who held a doctorate in classical literature from the University of Siena, thought that Margarito had been with other lions that day and was carrying their scent. Aside from that reasoning, which was invalid, he could think of no other explanation.

"In any event," he said, "they are roars of compassion, not battle."

And yet what most affected the tenor Ribero Silva was not that supernatural episode, but Margarito's confusion when they stopped to talk with the girls in the park. He remarked on it at the table, and we all agreed— some in order to make mischief and others because they were sympathetic—that it would be a good idea to help Margarito resolve his loneliness. Moved by our tender hearts, Bella Maria pressed her hands, covered by rings with imitation stones, against her bosom worthy of a doting biblical matriarch.

"I would do it for charity's sake," she said, "except that I never could abide men who wear vests."

That was how the tenor rode his Vespa to the Villa Borghese at two in the afternoon and returned with the little butterfly he thought best able to give Margarito Duarte an hour of good company. He had her undress in his bedroom, bathed her with scented soap, dried her, perfumed her with his personal cologne, and dusted her entire body with his camphorated aftershave talc. And then he paid her for the time they had already spent, plus another hour, and told her step by step what she had to do.

The naked beauty tiptoed through the shadowy house, like a siesta dream, gave two gentle little taps at the rear bedroom door, and Margarito Duarte appeared, barefoot and shirtless.

"*Buona sera, giovanotto,*" she said, with the voice and manners of a schoolgirl. "*Mi manda il tenore.*"

Margarito absorbed the shock with great dignity. He opened the door wide to let her in, and she lay down on the bed while he rushed to put on his shirt and shoes to receive her with all due respect. Then he sat beside her on a chair and began the conversation. The bewildered girl told him to hurry because they only had an hour. He did not seem to understand.

The girl said later that in any event she would have spent all the time he wanted and not charged him a cent, because there could not be a better behaved man anywhere in the world. Not knowing what to do in the meantime, she glanced around the room and saw the wooden case near the fireplace. She asked if it was a saxophone. Margarito did not answer, but opened the blind to let in a little light, carried the case to the bed, and raised the lid. The girl tried to say something, but her jaw was hanging open. Or as she told us later: "*Mi si gelò il culo*." She fled in utter terror, but lost her way in the hall and ran into Aunt Antonietta, who was going to my room to replace a light bulb. They were both so frightened that the girl did not dare leave the tenor's room until very late that night.

Aunt Antonietta never learned what happened. She came into my room in such fear that she could not turn the bulb in the lamp because her hands were shaking. I asked her what was wrong. "There are ghosts in this house," she said. "And now in broad daylight." She told me with great conviction that during the war a German officer had cut the throat of his mistress in the room occupied by the tenor. As Aunt Antonietta went about her work, she often saw the ghost of the beautiful victim making her way along the corridors.

"I've just seen her walking naked down the hall," she said. "She was identical."

The city resumed its autumn routine. The flowering terraces of summer closed down with the first winds, and the tenor and I returned to our old haunts in Trastevere, where we ate supper with the vocal students of Count Carlo Calcagni, and with some of my classmates from the film school, among whom the most faithful was Lakis, an intelligent, amiable Greek whose soporific discourses on social injustice were his only fault. It was our good fortune that the tenors and sopranos almost always drowned him out with operatic selections that they sang at full volume, but which did not bother anyone, even after midnight. On the contrary, some late-night passersby would join in the chorus, and neighbors opened their windows to applaud.

One night, while we were singing, Margarito tiptoed in so as not to interrupt us. He was carrying the pine case that he had not had time to leave at the *pensione* after showing the Saint to the parish priest at San Giovanni in Laterano, whose influence with the Holy Congregation of the Rite was common knowledge. From the corner of my eye I caught a glimpse of him putting it under the isolated table where he sat until we finished singing. As always, just after midnight, when the trattoria began to empty, we would push several tables together and sit in one group—those who sang, those of us who talked about movies, and all our friends. And among them Margarito Duarte, who was already known there as the silent, melancholy Colombian whose life was a mystery. Lakis was intrigued and asked him if he played the cello. I was caught off guard by what seemed to me an indiscretion too difficult to handle. The tenor was just as uncomfortable and could not save the situation. Margarito was the only one who responded to the question with absolute naturalness.

"It's not a cello," he said. "It's the Saint."

He placed the case on the table, opened the padlock, and raised the lid. A gust of stupefaction shook the restaurant. The other customers, the waiters, even the people in the kitchen with their bloodstained aprons, gathered in astonishment to see the miracle. Some crossed themselves. One of the cooks, overcome by a feverish trembling, fell to her knees with clasped hands and prayed in silence.

And yet when the initial commotion was over, we became involved in a shouting argument about the lack of saintliness in our day. Lakis, of course, was the most radical. The only clear idea at the end of it was that he wanted to make a critical movie about the Saint.

"I'm sure," he said, "that old Cesare would never let this subject get away."

He was referring to Cesare Zavattini, who taught us plot development and screenwriting. He was one of the great figures in the history of film, and the only one who maintained a personal relationship with us outside class. He tried to teach us not only the craft but a different way of looking at life. He was a machine for inventing plots. They poured out of him, almost against his will, and with such speed that he always needed someone to help catch them in mid-flight as he thought them up aloud. His enthusiasm would flag only when he had completed them. "Too bad they have to be filmed," he would say. For he thought that on the screen they would lose much of their original magic. He kept his ideas on cards arranged by subject and pinned to the walls, and he had so many they filled an entire room in his house.

The following Saturday we took Margarito Duarte to see him. Zavattini was so greedy for life that we found him at the door of his house on the Via di Sant'-Angela Merici, burning with interest in the idea we had described to him on the telephone. He did not even greet us with his customary amiability, but led Margarito to a table he had prepared, and opened the case himself. Then something happened that we never could have imagined. Instead of going wild, as we expected, he suffered a kind of mental paralysis.

"*Ammazza!*" he whispered in fear.

He looked at the Saint in silence for two or three minutes, closed the case himself, and without saying a word led Margarito to the door as if he were a child taking his first steps. He said good-bye with a few pats on his shoulder. "Thank you, my son, thank you very much," he said. "And may God be with you in your struggle." When he closed the door he turned toward us and gave his verdict.

"It's no good for the movies," he said. "Nobody would believe it."

That surprising lesson rode with us on the streetcar we took home. If he said it, it had to be true: The story was no good. Yet Bella Maria met us at the *pensione* with the urgent message that Zavattini was expecting us that same night, but without Margarito.

We found the maestro in one of his stellar moments. Lakis had brought along two or three classmates, but he did not even seem to see them when he opened the door.

"I have it," he shouted. "The picture will be a sensation if Margarito performs a miracle and resurrects the girl."

"In the picture or in life?" I asked.

He suppressed his annoyance. "Don't be stupid," he

said. But then we saw in his eyes the flash of an irresistible idea. "What if he could resurrect her in real life?" he mused, and added in all seriousness:

"He ought to try."

It was no more than a passing temptation, and then he took up the thread again. He began to pace every room, like a happy lunatic, waving his hands and reciting the film in great shouts. We listened to him, dazzled, and it seemed we could see the images, like flocks of phosphorescent birds that he set loose for their mad flight through the house.

"One night," he said, "after something like twenty popes who refused to receive him have died, Margarito grown old and tired goes into his house, opens the case, caresses the face of the little dead girl, and says with all the tenderness in the world: 'For love of your father, my child, arise and walk.'"

He looked at all of us and finished with a triumphant gesture:

"And she does!"

He was waiting for something from us. But we were so befuddled we could not think of a thing to say. Except Lakis the Greek, who raised his hand, as if he were in school, to ask permission to speak.

"My problem is that I don't believe it," he said, and to our surprise he was speaking to Zavattini: "Excuse me, Maestro, but I don't believe it."

Then it was Zavattini's turn to be astonished.

"And why not?"

"How do I know?" said Lakis in anguish. "But it's impossible."

"*Ammazza!*" the maestro thundered in a voice that must have been heard throughout the entire neighborhood. "That's what I can't stand about Stalinists: They don't believe in reality."

For the next fifteen years, as he himself told me, Margarito carried the Saint to Castel Gandolfo in the event an opportunity arose for displaying her. At an audience for some two hundred pilgrims from Latin America, he managed to tell his story, amid shoves and pokes, to the benevolent John XXIII. But he could not show him the girl because, as a precaution against assassination attempts, he had been obliged to leave her at the entrance along with the knapsacks of the other pilgrims. The Pope listened with as much attention as he could in the crowd, and gave him an encouraging pat on the cheek.

"*Bravo, figlio mio*," he said. "God will reward your perseverance."

But it was during the fleeting reign of the smiling Albino Luciani that Margarito really felt on the verge of fulfilling his dream. One of the Pope's relatives, impressed by Margarito's story, promised to intervene. No one paid him much attention. But two days later, as they were having lunch at the *pensione*, someone telephoned with a simple, rapid message for Margarito: He should not leave Rome, because sometime before Thursday he would be summoned to the Vatican for a private audience.

No one ever found out whether it was a joke. Margarito did not think so and stayed on the alert. He did not leave the house. If he had to go to the bathroom he announced: "I'm going to the bathroom." Bella Maria, still witty in the dawn of her old age, laughed her free woman's laugh.

"We know, Margarito," she shouted, "just in case the Pope calls."

Early one morning the following week Margarito almost collapsed when he saw the headline in the newspaper slipped under the door: *"Morto il Papa."* For a moment he was sustained by the illusion that it was an old paper delivered by mistake, since it was not easy to believe that a pope would die every month. But it was true: The smiling Albino Luciani, elected thirty-three days earlier, had died in his sleep.

I returned to Rome twenty-two years after I first met Margarito Duarte, and perhaps I would not have thought about him at all if we had not run into each other by accident. I was too depressed by the ruinous weather to think about anybody. An imbecilic drizzle like warm soup never stopped falling, the diamond light of another time had turned muddy, and the places that had once been mine and sustained my memories were strange to me now. The building where the *pensione* was located had not changed, but nobody knew anything about Bella Maria. No one answered at the six different telephone numbers that the tenor Ribero Silva had sent me over the years. At lunch with new movie people, I evoked the memory of my teacher, and a sudden silence fluttered over the table for a moment until someone dared to say:

"Zavattini? Mai sentito."

That was true: No one had heard of him. The trees in the Villa Borghese were disheveled in the rain, the *galop-*

patoio of the sorrowful princesses had been devoured by weeds without flowers, and the beautiful girls of long ago had been replaced by athletic androgynes cross-dressed in flashy clothes. Among all the extinct fauna, the only survivor was the old lion, who suffered from mange and a head cold on his island surrounded by dried waters. No one sang or died of love in the plastic trattorias on the Piazza di Spagna. For the Rome of our memory was by now another ancient Rome within the ancient Rome of the Caesars. Then a voice that might have come from the beyond stopped me cold on a narrow street in Trastevere:

"Hello, Poet."

It was he, old and tired. Four popes had died, eternal Rome was showing the first signs of decrepitude, and still he waited. "I've waited so long it can't be much longer now," he told me as he said good-bye after almost four hours of nostalgia. "It may be a matter of months." He shuffled down the middle of the street, wearing the combat boots and faded cap of an old Roman, ignoring the puddles of rain where the light was beginning to decay. Then I had no doubt, if I ever had any at all, that the Saint was Margarito. Without realizing it, by means of his daughter's incorruptible body and while he was still alive, he had spent twenty-two years fighting for the legitimate cause of his own canonization.

AUGUST 1981

Sleeping Beauty
and the Airplane

SHE WAS BEAUTIFUL and lithe, with soft skin the color of bread and eyes like green almonds, and she had straight black hair that reached to her shoulders, and an aura of antiquity that could just as well have been Indonesian as Andean. She was dressed with subtle taste: a lynx jacket, a raw silk blouse with very delicate flowers, natural linen trousers, and shoes with a narrow stripe the color of bougainvillea. "This is the most beautiful woman I've ever seen," I thought when I saw her pass by with the stealthy stride of a lioness while I waited in the check-in line at Charles de Gaulle Airport in Paris for the plane to New York. She was a supernatural apparition who existed only for a moment and disappeared into the crowd in the terminal.

It was nine in the morning. It had been snowing all night, and traffic was heavier than usual in the city streets, and even slower on the highway, where trailer trucks were lined up on the shoulder and automobiles steamed in the snow. Inside the airport terminal, however, it was still spring.

I stood behind an old Dutch woman who spent almost an hour arguing about the weight of her eleven suitcases. I was beginning to feel bored when I saw the momentary apparition who left me breathless, and so I never knew how the dispute ended. Then the ticket clerk brought me down from the clouds with a reproach for my distraction. By way of an excuse, I asked her if she believed in love at first sight. "Of course," she said. "The other kinds are impossible." She kept her eyes fixed on the computer screen and asked whether I preferred a seat in smoking or nonsmoking.

"It doesn't matter," I said with intentional malice, "as long as I'm not beside the eleven suitcases."

She expressed her appreciation with a commercial smile but did not look away from the glowing screen.

"Choose a number," she told me: "Three, four, or seven."

"Four."

Her smile flashed in triumph.

"In the fifteen years I've worked here," she said, "you're the first person who hasn't chosen seven."

She wrote the seat number on my boarding pass and returned it with the rest of my papers, looking at me for the first time with grape-colored eyes that were a consolation until I could see Beauty again. Only then did she inform me that the airport had just been closed and all flights delayed.

"For how long?"

"That's up to God," she said with her smile. "The radio said this morning it would be the biggest snowstorm of the year."

She was wrong: It was the biggest of the century. But in the first-class waiting room, spring was so real that there were live roses in the vases and even the canned music seemed as sublime and tranquilizing as its creators had intended. All at once it occurred to me that this was a suitable shelter for Beauty, and I looked for her in the other waiting areas, staggered by my own boldness. But most of the people were men from real life who read newspapers in English while their wives thought about someone else as they looked through the panoramic windows at the planes dead in the snow, the glacial factories, the vast fields of Roissy devastated by fierce lions. By noon there was no place to sit, and the heat had become so unbearable that I escaped for a breath of air.

Outside I saw an overwhelming sight. All kinds of people had crowded into the waiting rooms and were camped in the stifling corridors and even on the stairways, stretched out on the floor with their animals, their children, and their travel gear. Communication with the city had also been interrupted, and the palace of transparent plastic resembled an immense space capsule stranded in the storm. I could not help thinking that Beauty too must be somewhere in the middle of those tamed hordes, and the fantasy inspired me with new courage to wait.

By lunchtime we had realized that we were shipwrecked. The lines were interminable outside the seven restaurants, the cafeterias, the packed bars, and in less than three hours they all had to be closed because there was nothing left to eat or drink. The children, who for a moment seemed to be all the children in the world, started to cry at the same time, and a herd smell began to rise from the crowd. It was a time for instinct. In all that scrambling, the only thing I could find to eat were the last two cups of vanilla ice cream in a children's shop. The waiters were putting chairs on tables as the patrons left, while I ate very slowly at the counter, seeing myself in the mirror with the last little cardboard cup and the last little cardboard spoon, and thinking about Beauty.

The flight to New York, scheduled for eleven in the morning, left at eight that night. By the time I managed to board, the other first-class passengers were already in their seats, and a flight attendant led me to mine. My heart stopped. In the seat next to mine, beside the window, Beauty was taking possession of her space with the mastery of an expert traveler. "If I ever wrote this, nobody would believe me," I thought. And I just managed to stammer an indecisive greeting that she did not hear.

She settled in as if she were going to live there for many years, putting each thing in its proper place and order, until her seat was arranged like the ideal house, where everything was within reach. In the meantime, a steward brought us our welcoming champagne. I took a glass to offer to her, but thought better of it just in time. For she wanted only a glass of water, and she asked the steward, first in incomprehensible French and then in an English only somewhat more fluent, not to wake her for any reason during the flight. Her warm, serious voice was tinged with Oriental sadness.

When he brought the water, she placed a cosmetics case with copper corners, like a grandmother's trunk, on her lap, and took two golden pills from a box that contained others of various colors. She did everything in a methodical, solemn way, as if nothing unforeseen had happened to her since her birth. At last she pulled down the shade on the window, lowered the back of her seat as far as it would go, covered herself to the waist with a blanket without taking off her shoes, put on a sleeping mask, turned her back to me, and then slept without a single pause, without a sigh, without the slightest change in position, for the eight eternal hours and twelve extra minutes of the flight to New York.

It was an ardent journey. I have always believed that there is nothing more beautiful in nature than a beautiful woman, and it was impossible for me to escape even for a moment from the spell of that storybook creature who slept at my side. The steward disappeared as soon as we took off and was replaced by a Cartesian attendant who tried to awaken Beauty to hand her a toiletry case and a set of earphones for listening to music. I repeated the instructions she had given the steward, but the attendant insisted on hearing from Beauty's own lips that she did not want supper either. The steward had to confirm her instructions, and even so he reproached me because Beauty had not hung the little cardboard "Do Not Disturb" sign around her neck.

I ate a solitary supper, telling myself in silence everything I would have told her if she had been awake. Her sleep was so steady that at one point I had the distressing thought that the pills she had taken were not for sleeping but for dying. With each drink I raised my glass and toasted her.

"To your health, Beauty."

When supper was over the lights were dimmed and a movie was shown to no one, and the two of us were alone in the darkness of the world. The biggest storm of the century had ended, and the Atlantic night was immense and limpid, and the plane seemed motionless among the stars. Then I contemplated her, inch by inch, for several hours, and the only sign of life I could detact were the shadows of the dreams that passed along her forehead like clouds over water. Around her neck she wore a chain so fine it was almost invisible against her golden skin, her perfect ears were unpierced, her nails were rosy with good health, and on her left hand was a plain band. Since she looked no older than twenty, I consoled myself with the idea that it was not a wedding ring but the sign of an ephemeral engagement. "To know you are sleeping, certain, secure, faithful channel of renunciation, pure line, so close to my manacled arms," I thought on the foaming crest of champagne, repeating the masterful sonnet by Gerardo Diego. Then I lowered the back of my seat to the level of hers, and we lay together, closer than if we had been in a marriage bed. The climate of her breathing was the same as that of her voice, and her skin exhaled a delicate breath that could only be the scent of her beauty. It seemed incredible: The previous spring I had read a beautiful novel by Yasunari Kawabata about the ancient bourgeois of Kyoto who paid enormous sums to spend the night watching the most beautiful girls in the city, naked and drugged, while they agonized with love in the same bed. They could not wake them, or touch them, and they did not even try, because the essence of their pleasure was to see them sleeping. That night, as I watched over Beauty's sleep, I not only understood that senile refinement but lived it to the full.

"Who would have thought," I said to myself, my vanity exacerbated by champagne, "that I'd become an ancient Japanese at this late date."

I think I slept several hours, conquered by champagne and the mute explosions of the movie, and when I awoke my head was splitting. I went to the bathroom. Two seats behind mine the old woman with the eleven suitcases lay in an awkward sprawl, like a forgotten corpse on a battlefield. Her reading glasses, on a chain of colored beads, were on the floor in the middle of the aisle, and for a moment I enjoyed the malicious pleasure of not picking them up.

After I got rid of the excesses of champagne, I caught sight of myself, contemptible and ugly, in the mirror, and was amazed that the devastation of love could be so terrible. The plane lost altitude without warning, then managed to straighten out and continue full speed ahead. The "Return to Your Seat" sign went on. I hurried out with the hope that God's turbulence might awaken Beauty and she would have to take refuge in my arms to escape her terror. In my haste I almost stepped on the Dutchwoman's glasses and would have been happy if I had. But I retraced my steps, picked them up, and put them on her lap in sudden gratitude for her not having chosen seat number four before I did.

Beauty's sleep was invincible. When the plane stabilized, I had to resist the temptation to shake her on some pretext, because all I wanted in the last hour of the flight was to see her awake, even if she were furious, so that I could recover my freedom, and perhaps my youth. But I couldn't do it. "Damn it," I said to myself with great scorn. "Why wasn't I born a Taurus!"

She awoke by herself at the moment the landing lights went on, and she was as beautiful and refreshed as if she had slept in a rose garden. That was when I realized that like old married couples, people who sit next to each other on airplanes do not say good morning to each other when they wake up. Nor did she. She took off her mask, opened her radiant eyes, straightened the back of the seat, moved the blanket aside, shook her hair that fell into place of its own weight, put the cosmetics case back on her knees, and applied rapid, unnecessary makeup, which took just enough time so that she did not look at me until the plane door opened. Then she put on her lynx jacket, almost stepped over me with a conventional excuse in pure Latin American Spanish, left without even saying good-bye or at least thanking me for all I had done to make our night together a happy one, and disappeared into the sun of today in the Amazon jungle of New York.

JUNE 1982

I Sell My Dreams

O NE MORNING at nine o'clock, while we were having breakfast on the terrace of the Havana Riviera Hotel under a bright sun, a huge wave picked up several cars that were driving down the avenue along the seawall or parked on the pavement, and embedded one of them in the side of the hotel. It was like an explosion of dynamite that sowed panic on all twenty floors of the building and turned the great entrance window to dust. The many tourists in the lobby were thrown into the air along with the furniture, and some were cut by the hailstorm of glass. The wave must have been immense, because it leaped over the wide two-way street between the seawall and the hotel and still had enough force to shatter the window.

The cheerful Cuban volunteers, with the help of the fire department, picked up the debris in less than six hours, and sealed off the gate to the sea and installed another, and everything returned to normal. During the morning nobody worried about the car encrusted in the wall, for people assumed it was one of those that had been parked on the pavement. But when the crane lifted it out of its setting, the body of a woman was found secured behind the steering wheel by a seat belt. The blow had been so brutal that not a single one of her bones was left whole. Her face was destroyed, her boots had been ripped apart, and her clothes were in shreds. She wore a gold ring shaped like a serpent, with emerald eyes. The police established that she was the housekeeper for the new Portuguese ambassador and his wife. She had come to Havana with them two weeks before and had left that morning for the market, driving a new car. Her name meant nothing to me when I read it in the newspaper, but I was intrigued by the snake ring and its emerald eyes. I could not find out, however, on which finger she wore it.

This was a crucial piece of information, because I feared she was an unforgettable woman whose real name I never knew, and who wore a similar ring on her right forefinger, which in those days was even more unusual than it is now. I had met her thirty-four years earlier in Vienna, eating sausage with boiled potatoes and drinking draft beer in a tavern frequented by Latin American students. I had come from Rome that morning, and I still remember my immediate response to her splendid soprano's bosom, the languid foxtails on her coat collar, and that Egyptian ring in the shape of a serpent. She spoke an elementary Spanish in a metallic accent without pausing for breath, and I thought she was the only Austrian at the long wooden table. But no, she had been born in Colombia and had come to Austria between the wars, when she was little more than a child, to study music and voice. She was about thirty, and did not carry her years well, for she had never been pretty and had begun to age before her time. But she was a charming human being. And one of the most awe-inspiring.

Vienna was still an old imperial city, whose geographical position between the two irreconcilable worlds left behind by the Second World War had turned it into a paradise of black marketeering and international espionage. I could not have imagined a more suitable spot for my fugitive compatriot, who still ate in the students' tavern on the corner only out of loyalty to her origins, since she had more than enough money to buy meals for all her table companions. She never told her real name, and we always knew her by the Germanic tongue twister that we Latin American students in Vienna invented for her: Frau Frieda. I had just been introduced to her when I committed the happy impertinence of asking how she had come to be in a world so distant and different from the windy cliffs of Quindío, and she answered with a devastating:

"I sell my dreams."

In reality, that was her only trade. She had been the third of eleven children born to a prosperous shopkeeper in old Caldas, and as soon as she learned to speak she instituted the fine custom in her family of telling dreams before breakfast, the time when their oracular qualities are preserved in their purest form. When she was seven she dreamed that one of her brothers was carried off by a flood. Her mother, out of sheer religious superstition, forbade the boy to swim in the ravine, which was his favorite pastime. But Frau Frieda already had her own system of prophecy.

"What that dream means," she said, "isn't that he's going to drown, but that he shouldn't eat sweets."

Her interpretation seemed an infamy to a five-year-old boy who could not live without his Sunday treats. Their mother, convinced of her daughter's oracular talents, enforced the warning with an iron hand. But in her first careless moment the boy choked on a piece of caramel that he was eating in secret, and there was no way to save him.

Frau Frieda did not think she could earn a living with her talent until life caught her by the throat during the cruel Viennese winters. Then she looked for work at the first house where she would have liked to live, and when she was asked what she could do, she told only the truth: "I dream." A brief explanation to the lady of the house was all she needed, and she was hired at a salary that just covered her minor expenses, but she had a nice room and three meals a day—breakfast in particular, when the family sat down to learn the immediate future of each of its members: the father, a refined financier; the mother, a joyful woman passionate about Romantic chamber music; and two children, eleven and nine years old. They were all religious and therefore inclined to archaic superstitions, and they were delighted to take in Frau Frieda, whose only obligation was to decipher the family's daily fate through her dreams.

She did her job well, and for a long time, above all during the war years, when reality was more sinister than nightmares. Only she could decide at breakfast what each should do that day, and how it should be done, until her predictions became the sole authority in the house. Her control over the family was absolute: Even the faintest sigh was breathed by her order. The master of the house died at about the time I was in Vienna, and had the elegance to leave her a part of his estate on the condition that she continue dreaming for the family until her dreams came to an end.

I stayed in Vienna for more than a month, sharing the straitened circumstances of the other students while I waited for money that never arrived. Frau Frieda's unexpected and generous visits to the tavern were like fiestas in our poverty-stricken regime. One night, in a beery euphoria, she whispered in my ear with a conviction that permitted no delay.

"I only came to tell you that I dreamed about you last night," she said. "You must leave right away and not come back to Vienna for five years."

Her conviction was so real that I boarded the last train to Rome that same night. As for me, I was so influenced by what she said that from then on I considered myself a survivor of some catastrophe I never experienced. I still have not returned to Vienna.

Before the disaster in Havana, I had seen Frau Frieda in Barcelona in so unexpected and fortuitous a way that it seemed a mystery to me. It happened on the day Pablo Neruda stepped on Spanish soil for the first time since the Civil War, on a stopover during a long sea voyage to Valparaíso. He spent a morning with us hunting big game in the secondhand bookstores, and at Porter he bought an old, dried-out volume with a torn binding for which he paid what would have been his salary for two months at the consulate in Rangoon. He moved through the crowd like an invalid elephant, with a child's curiosity in the inner workings of each thing he saw, for the world appeared to him as an immense wind-up toy with which life invented itself.

I have never known anyone closer to the idea one has of a Renaissance pope: He was gluttonous and refined. Even against his will, he always presided at the table. Matilde, his wife, would put a bib around his neck that belonged in a barbershop rather than a dining room, but it was the only way to keep him from taking a bath in sauce. That day at Carvalleiras was typical. He ate three whole lobsters, dissecting them with a surgeon's skill, and at the same time devoured everyone else's plate with his eyes and tasted a little from each with a delight that made the desire to eat contagious: clams from Galicia, mussels from Cantabria, prawns from Alicante, sea cucumbers from the Costa Brava. In the meantime, like the French, he spoke of nothing but other culinary delicacies, in particular the prehistoric shellfish of Chile, which he carried in his heart. All at once he stopped eating, tuned his lobster's antennae, and said to me in a very quiet voice:

"There's someone behind me who won't stop looking at me."

I glanced over his shoulder, and it was true. Three tables away sat an intrepid woman in an old-fashioned felt hat and a purple scarf, eating without haste and staring at him. I recognized her right away. She had grown old and fat, but it was Frau Frieda, with the snake ring on her index finger.

She was traveling from Naples on the same ship as Neruda and his wife, but they had not seen each other on board. We invited her to have coffee at our table, and I encouraged her to talk about her dreams in order to astound the poet. He paid no attention, for from the very beginning he had announced that he did not believe in prophetic dreams.

"Only poetry is clairvoyant," he said.

After lunch, during the inevitable stroll along the Ramblas, I lagged behind with Frau Frieda so that we could renew our memories with no other ears listening. She told me she had sold her properties in Austria and retired to Oporto, in Portugal, where she lived in a house that she described as a fake castle on a hill, from which one could see all the way across the ocean to the Americas. Although she did not say so, her conversation made it clear that, dream by dream, she had taken over the entire fortune of her ineffable patrons in Vienna. That did not surprise me, however, because I had always thought her dreams were no more than a stratagem for surviving. And I told her so.

She laughed her irresistible laugh. "You're as impudent as ever," she said. And said no more, because the rest of the group had stopped to wait for Neruda to finish talking in Chilean slang to the parrots along the Rambla de los Pájaros. When we resumed our conversation, Frau Frieda changed the subject.

"By the way," she said, "you can go back to Vienna now."

Only then did I realize that thirteen years had gone by since our first meeting.

"Even if your dreams are false, I'll never go back," I told her. "Just in case."

At three o'clock we left her to accompany Neruda to his sacred siesta, which he took in our house after solemn preparations that in some way recalled the Japanese tea ceremony. Some windows had to be opened and others closed to achieve the perfect degree of warmth, and there had to be a certain kind of light from a certain direction, and absolute silence. Neruda fell asleep right away, and woke ten minutes later, as children do, when we least expected it. He appeared in the living room refreshed, and with the monogram of the pillowcase imprinted on his cheek.

"I dreamed about that woman who dreams," he said.

Matilde wanted him to tell her his dream.

"I dreamed she was dreaming about me," he said.

"That's right out of Borges," I said.

He looked at me in disappointment.

"Has he written it already?"

"If he hasn't he'll write it sometime," I said. "It will be one of his labyrinths."

As soon as he boarded the ship at six that evening, Neruda took his leave of us, sat down at an isolated table, and began to write fluid verses in the green ink he used for drawing flowers and fish and birds when he dedicated his books. At the first "All ashore" we looked for Frau

Frieda, and found her at last on the tourist deck, just as we were about to leave without saying good-bye. She too had taken a siesta.

"I dreamed about the poet," she said.

In astonishment I asked her to tell me her dream.

"I dreamed he was dreaming about me," she said, and my look of amazement disconcerted her. "What did you expect? Sometimes, with all my dreams, one slips in that has nothing to do with real life."

I never saw her again or even wondered about her until I heard about the snake ring on the woman who died in the Havana Riviera disaster. And I could not resist the temptation of questioning the Portuguese ambassador when we happened to meet some months later at a diplomatic reception. The ambassador spoke about her with great enthusiasm and enormous admiration. "You cannot imagine how extraordinary she was," he said. "You would have been obliged to write a story about her." And he went on in the same tone, with surprising details, but without the clue that would have allowed me to come to a final conclusion.

"In concrete terms," I asked at last, "what did she do?"

"Nothing," he said, with a certain disenchantment. "She dreamed."

MARCH 1980

70

"I Only Came
to Use the Phone"

ONE RAINY spring afternoon, while María de la
Luz Cervantes was driving alone back to Barcelona, her
rented car broke down in the Monegros desert. She was
twenty-seven years old, a thoughtful, pretty Mexican
who had enjoyed a certain fame as a music hall performer
a few years earlier. She was married to a cabaret magician,
whom she was to meet later that day after visiting some
relatives in Zaragoza. For an hour she made desperate
signals to the cars and trucks that sped past her in the
storm, until at last the driver of a ramshackle bus took
pity on her. He did warn her, however, that he was not
going very far.

"It doesn't matter," said María. "All I need is a telephone."

That was true, and she needed it only to let her husband

71

know that she would not be home before seven. Wearing a student's coat and beach shoes in April, she looked like a bedraggled little bird, and she was so distraught after her mishap that she forgot to take the car keys. A woman with a military air was sitting next to the driver, and she gave María a towel and a blanket and made room for her on the seat. María wiped off the worst of the rain and then sat down, wrapped herself in the blanket, and tried to light a cigarette, but her matches were wet. The woman sharing the seat gave her a light and asked for one of the few cigarettes that were still dry. While they smoked, María gave in to a desire to vent her feelings and raised her voice over the noise of the rain and the clatter of the bus. The woman interrupted her by placing a forefinger to her lips.

"They're asleep," she whispered.

María looked over her shoulder and saw that the bus was full of women of uncertain ages and varying conditions who were sleeping in blankets just like hers. Their serenity was contagious, and María curled up in her seat and succumbed to the sound of the rain. When she awoke, it was dark and the storm had dissolved into an icy drizzle. She had no idea how long she had slept or what place in the world they had come to. Her neighbor looked watchful.

"Where are we?" María asked.

"We've arrived," answered the woman.

The bus was entering the cobbled courtyard of an enormous, gloomy building that seemed to be an old convent in a forest of colossal trees. The passengers, just visible in the dim light of a lamp in the courtyard, sat

motionless until the woman with the military air ordered
them out of the bus with the kind of primitive directions
used in nursery school. They were all older women, and
their movements were so lethargic in the half-light of the
courtyard that they looked like images in a dream. María,
the last to climb down, thought they were nuns. She was
less certain when she saw several women in uniform who
received them at the door of the bus, pulled the blankets
over their heads to keep them dry, and lined them up single file, directing them not by speaking but with rhyth-
mic, peremptory clapping. María said good-bye and tried
to give the blanket to the woman whose seat she had
shared, but the woman told her to use it to cover her head
while she crossed the courtyard and then return it at the
porter's office.

"Is there a telephone?" María asked.

"Of course," said the woman. "They'll show you
where it is."

She asked for another cigarette, and María gave her
the rest of the damp pack. "They'll dry on the way,"
she said. The woman waved good-bye from the running
board, and called "Good luck" in a voice that was almost
a shout. The bus pulled away without giving her time to
say anything else.

María started running toward the doorway of the
building. A matron tried to stop her with an energetic
clap of the hands, but had to resort to an imperious shout:
"Stop, I said!" María looked out from under the blanket
and saw a pair of icy eyes and an inescapable forefinger
pointing her into the line. She obeyed. Once inside the
vestibule she separated from the group and asked the

porter where the telephone was. One of the matrons returned her to the line with little pats on the shoulder while she said in a saccharine voice:

"This way, beautiful, the telephone's this way."

María walked with the other women down a dim corridor until they came to a communal dormitory, where the matrons collected the blankets and began to assign beds. Another matron, who seemed more humane and of higher rank to María, walked down the line comparing a list of names with those written on cardboard tags stitched to the bodices of the new arrivals. When she reached María, she was surprised to see that she was not wearing her identification.

"I only came to use the phone," María told her.

She explained with great urgency that her car had broken down on the highway. Her husband, who performed magic tricks at parties, was waiting for her in Barcelona because they had three engagements before midnight, and she wanted to let him know she would not be there in time to go with him. It was almost seven o'clock. He had to leave home in ten minutes, and she was afraid he would cancel everything because she was late. The matron appeared to listen to her with attention.

"What's your name?" she asked.

María said her name with a sigh of relief, but the woman did not find it after going over the list several times. With some alarm she questioned another matron, who had nothing to say and shrugged her shoulders.

"But I only came to use the phone," said María.

"Sure, honey," the supervisor told her, escorting her to her bed with a sweetness that was too patent to be real, "if you're good you can call anybody you want. But not now, tomorrow."

Then something clicked in María's mind, and she understood why the women on the bus moved as if they were on the bottom of an aquarium. They were, in fact, sedated with tranquilizers, and that dark palace with the thick stone walls and frozen stairways was really a hospital for female mental patients. She raced out of the dormitory in dismay, but before she could reach the main door a gigantic matron wearing mechanic's coveralls stopped her with a blow of her huge hand and held her immobile on the floor in an armlock. María, paralyzed with terror, looked at her sideways.

"For the love of God," she said. "I swear by my dead mother I only came to use the phone."

Just one glance at her face was enough for María to know that no amount of pleading would move that maniac in coveralls who was called Herculina because of her uncommon strength. She was in charge of difficult cases, and two inmates had been strangled to death by her polar bear arm skilled in the art of killing by mistake. It was established that the first case had been an accident. The second proved less clear, and Herculina was admonished and warned that the next time she would be subjected to a thorough investigation. The accepted story was that this black sheep of a fine old family had a dubious history of suspicious accidents in various mental hospitals throughout Spain.

They had to inject María with a sedative to make her sleep the first night. When a longing to smoke roused her before dawn, she was tied to the metal bars of the bed by her wrists and ankles. She shouted, but no one came. In the morning, while her husband could find no trace of her in Barcelona, she had to be taken to the infirmary, for they found her senseless in a swamp of her own misery.

When she regained consciousness she did not know how much time had passed. But now the world seemed a haven of love. Beside her bed, a monumental old man with a flat-footed walk and a calming smile gave her back her joy in being alive with two masterful passes of his hand. He was the director of the sanatorium.

Before saying anything to him, without even greeting him, María asked for a cigarette. He lit one and handed it to her, along with the pack, which was almost full. María could not hold back her tears.

"Now is the time to cry to your heart's content," the doctor said in a soporific voice. "Tears are the best medicine."

María unburdened herself without shame, as she had never been able to do with her casual lovers in the empty times that followed lovemaking. As he listened, the doctor smoothed her hair with his fingers, arranged her pillow to ease her breathing, guided her through the labyrinth of her uncertainty with a wisdom and a sweetness she never had dreamed possible. This was, for the first time in her life, the miracle of being understood by a man who listened to her with all his heart and did not expect to go to bed with her as a reward. At the end of a long hour, when she had bared the depths of her soul, she asked permission to speak to her husband on the telephone.

The doctor stood up with all the majesty of his position. "Not yet, princess," he said, patting her cheek

76

with more tenderness than she ever had felt before. "Everything in due course." He gave her a bishop's blessing from the door, asked her to trust him, and disappeared forever.

That same afternoon María was admitted to the asylum with a serial number and a few superficial comments concerning the enigma of where she had come from and the doubts surrounding her identity. In the margin the director had written an assessment in his own hand: *agitated*.

Just as María had foreseen, her husband left their modest apartment in the Horta district half an hour behind schedule for his three engagements. It was the first time she had been late in the almost two years of their free and very harmonious union, and he assumed it was due to the heavy downpours that had devastated the entire province that weekend. Before he went out he pinned a note to the door with his itinerary for the night.

At the first party, where all the children were dressed in kangaroo costumes, he omitted his best illusion, the invisible fish, because he could not do it without her assistance. His second engagement was in the house of a ninety-three-year-old woman in a wheelchair, who prided herself on having celebrated each of her last thirty birthdays with a different magician. He was so troubled by María's absence that he could not concentrate on the simplest tricks. At his third engagement, the one he did every night at a café on the Ramblas, he gave an uninspired performance for a group of French tourists who could not believe what they saw because they refused to believe in magic. After each show he telephoned his house, and waited in despair for María to answer. After the last call he could no longer control his concern that something had happened to her.

On his way home, in the van adapted for public performances, he saw the splendor of spring in the palm trees along the Paseo de Gracia, and he shuddered at the ominous thought of what the city would be like without María. His last hope vanished when he found his note still pinned to the door. He was so troubled he forgot to feed the cat.

I realize now as I write this that I never learned his real name, because in Barcelona we knew him only by his professional name: Saturno the Magician. He was a man of odd character and irredeemable social awkwardness, but María had more than enough of the tact and charm he lacked. It was she who led him by the hand through this community of great mysteries, where no man would have dreamed of calling after midnight to look for his wife. Saturno had, soon after he arrived, and he preferred to forget the incident. And so that night he settled for calling Zaragoza, where a sleepy grandmother told him with no alarm that María had said goodbye after lunch. He slept for just an hour at dawn. He had a muddled dream in which he saw María wearing a ragged wedding dress spattered with blood, and he woke with the fearful certainty that this time she had left him forever, to face the vast world without her.

She had deserted three different men, including him, in the last five years. She had left him in Mexico City six months after they met, when they were in the throes of pleasure from their demented lovemaking in a maid's room in the Anzures district. One morning, after a night of unspeakable profligacy, María was gone. She left behind everything that was hers, even the ring from her previous marriage, along with a letter in which she said she was incapable of surviving the torment of that wild love. Saturno thought she had returned to her first husband, a high school classmate she had married in secret while still a minor and abandoned for another man after two loveless years. But no: She had gone to her parents' house, and Saturno followed to get her back regardless of the cost. His pleading was unconditional, he made many more promises than he was prepared to keep, but he came up against an invincible determination. "There are short loves and there are long ones," she told him. And she concluded with a merciless, "This was a short one." Her inflexibility forced him to admit defeat. But in the early hours of the morning of All Saints' Day, when he returned to his orphan's room after almost a year of deliberate forgetting, he found her asleep on the living room sofa with the crown of orange blossoms and long tulle train worn by virgin brides.

María told him the truth. Her new fiancé, a childless widower with a settled life and a mind to marry forever in the Catholic Church, had left her dressed and waiting at the altar. Her parents decided to hold the reception anyway, and she played along with them. She danced, sang with the mariachis, had too much to drink, and in a terrible state of belated remorse left at midnight to find Saturno.

He was not home, but she found the keys in the flower pot in the hall, where they always hid them. Now she was the one whose surrender was unconditional. "How long this time?" he asked. She answered with a line by Vinicius de Moraes: "Love is eternal for as long as it lasts." Two years later, it was still eternal.

María seemed to mature. She renounced her dreams of being an actress and dedicated herself to him, both in work and in bed. At the end of the previous year they had attended a magicians' convention in Perpignan, and on their way home they visited Barcelona for the first time. They liked it so much they had been living here for eight months, and it suited them so well they bought an apartment in the very Catalonian neighborhood of Horta. It was noisy, and they had no porter, but there was more than enough room for five children. Their happiness was all one could hope for, until the weekend when she rented a car and went to visit her relatives in Zaragoza, promising to be back by seven on Monday night. By dawn on Thursday there was still no word from her.

On Monday of the following week, the insurance company for the rented car called and asked for María. "I don't know anything," said Saturno. "Look for her in Zaragoza." He hung up. A week later a police officer came to the house to report that the car had been found, stripped bare, on a back road to Cádiz, nine hundred kilometers from the spot where María had abandoned it. The officer wanted to know if she had further details regarding the theft. Saturno was feeding the cat, and he did not look up when he told him straight out that the police shouldn't waste their time because his wife had left him and he didn't know where she had gone or with whom. His conviction was so great that the officer felt uncom-

fortable and apologized for his questions. They declared
the case closed.

The suspicion that María might leave him again had
assailed Saturno at Easter in Cadaqués, where Rosa Regás had invited them to go sailing. In the Marítim, the
crowded, sordid bar of the *gauche divine* during the twilight of Francoism, twenty of us were squeezed together
around one of those wrought-iron tables that had room
only for six. After she smoked her second pack of cigarettes of the day, María ran out of matches. A thin, downy
arm wearing a Roman bronze bracelet made its way
through the noisy crowd at the table and gave her a light.
She said thank you without looking at the person she was
thanking, but Saturno the Magician saw him—a bony,
clean-shaven adolescent as pale as death, with a very black
ponytail that hung down to his waist. The windowpanes
in the bar just managed to withstand the fury of the
spring tramontana wind, but he wore a kind of street
pajama made of raw cotton, and a pair of farmer's sandals.

They did not see him again until late autumn, in a sea-
food bar in La Barceloneta, wearing the same plain cotton
outfit and a long braid instead of the ponytail. He greeted
them both as if they were old friends, and the way he
kissed María, and the way she kissed him back, struck
Saturno with the suspicion that they had been seeing
each other in secret. Days later he happened to come
across a new name and phone number that María had
written in their household address book, and the unmerciful lucidity of jealousy revealed to him whose they were.
The intruder's background was the final proof: He was

twenty-two years old, the only child of a wealthy family, and a decorator of fashionable shop windows, with a casual reputation as a bisexual and a well-founded notoriety as a paid comforter of married women. But Saturno managed to restrain himself until the night María did not come home. Then he began calling him every day, from six in the morning until just before the following dawn, every two or three hours at first, and then whenever he was near a telephone. The fact that no one answered intensified Saturno's martyrdom.

On the fourth day an Andalusian woman who was there just to clean picked up the phone. "The gentleman's gone away," she said, with enough vagueness to drive him mad. Saturno did not resist the temptation of asking if Señorita María was in by any chance.

"Nobody named María lives here," the woman told him. "The gentleman is a bachelor."

"I know," he said. "She doesn't live there, but sometimes she visits, right?"

The woman became annoyed.

"Who the hell is this, anyway?"

Saturno hung up. The woman's denial seemed one more confirmation of what for him was no longer a suspicion but a burning certainty. He lost control. In the days that followed he called everyone he knew in Barcelona, in alphabetical order. No one could tell him anything, but each call deepened his misery, because his jealous frenzies had become famous among the unrepentant night owls of the *gauche divine*, and they responded with any kind of joke that would make him suffer. Only then did he realize how alone he was in that beautiful, lunatic, impenetrable city, where he would never be happy. At dawn, after he fed the cat, he hardened his heart to keep from dying and resolved to forget María.

After two months María had not yet adjusted to life in the sanatorium. She survived by just picking at the prison rations with flatware chained to the long table of unfinished wood, her eyes fixed on the lithograph of General Francisco Franco that presided over the gloomy medieval dining room. At first she resisted the canonical hours with their mindless routine of matins, lauds, vespers, as well as the other church services that took up most of the time. She refused to play ball in the recreation yard, or to make artificial flowers in the workshop that a group of inmates attended with frenetic diligence. But after the third week she began, little by little, to join in the life of the cloister. After all, said the doctors, every one of them started out the same way, and sooner or later they became integrated into the community.

The lack of cigarettes, resolved in the first few days by a matron who sold them for the price of gold, returned to torment her again when she had spent the little money she had with her. Then she took comfort in the newspaper cigarettes that some inmates made with the butts they picked out of the trash, for her obsessive desire to smoke had become as intense as her fixation on the telephone. Later on, the few pesetas she earned making artificial flowers allowed her an ephemeral consolation.

Hardest of all was her loneliness at night. Many inmates lay awake in the semi-darkness, as she did, not daring to do anything because the night matron at the heavy door secured with a chain and padlock was awake too. One night, however, overcome with grief, María asked in a voice loud enough for the woman in the next bed to hear:

"Where are we?"

The grave, lucid voice of her neighbor answered:

"In the pit of hell."

"They say this is the country of the Moors," said another, distant voice that resounded throughout the dormitory. "And it must be true, because in the summer, when there's a moon, you can hear the dogs barking at the sea."

The chain running through the locks sounded like the anchor of a galleon, and the door opened. Their pitiless guardian, the only creature who seemed alive in the instantaneous silence, began walking from one end of the dormitory to the other. María was seized with terror, and only she knew why.

Since her first week in the sanatorium, the night matron had been proposing outright that María sleep with her in the guardroom. She began in a concrete, businesslike tone: an exchange of love for cigarettes, for chocolate, for whatever she wanted. "You'll have everything," the matron said, tremulous. "You'll be the queen." When María refused, she changed her tactics, leaving little love notes under her pillow, in the pockets of her robe, in the most unexpected places. They were messages of a heartbreaking urgency that could have moved a stone. On the night of the dormitory incident, it had been more than a month that she had seemed resigned to defeat.

When she was certain the other inmates were asleep, the matron approached María's bed and whispered all kinds of tender obscenities in her ear while she kissed her face, her neck tensed with terror, her rigid arms, her exhausted legs. Then, thinking perhaps that María's paralysis stemmed not from fear but from compliance, she dared to go further. That was when María hit her with the back of her hand and sent her crashing into the next bed. The enraged matron stood up in the midst of the uproar created by the agitated inmates.

"You bitch!" she shouted. "We'll rot together in this hellhole until you go crazy for me."

Summer arrived without warning on the first Sunday in June, requiring emergency measures because during Mass the sweltering inmates began taking off their shapeless serge gowns. With some amusement María watched the spectacle of naked patients being chased like blind chickens up and down the aisles by the matrons. In the confusion she tried to protect herself from wild blows, and she somehow found herself alone in an empty office, where the incessant ring of a telephone had a pleading tone. María answered without thinking and heard a distant, smiling voice that took great pleasure in imitating the telephone company's time service:

"The time is forty-five hours, ninety-two minutes, and one hundred seven seconds."

"Asshole," said María.

She hung up, amused. She was about to leave when she realized she was allowing a unique opportunity to slip away. She dialed six digits, with so much tension and so much haste she was not sure it was her home number. She waited, her heart racing, she heard the avid, sad sound of the familiar ring, once, twice, three times, and at last she heard the voice of the man she loved, in the house without her.

"Hello?"

She had to wait for the knot of tears that formed in her throat to dissolve.

"Baby, sweetheart," she sighed.

Her tears overcame her. On the other end of the line there was a brief, horrified silence, and a voice burning with jealousy spit out the word:

"Whore!"

And he slammed down the receiver.

That night, in an attack of rage, María pulled down the lithograph of the Generalissimo in the refectory, crashed it with all her strength into the stained-glass window that led to the garden, and threw herself to the floor, covered in blood. She still had enough fury left to resist the blows of the matrons who tried, with no success, to restrain her, until she saw Herculina standing in the doorway with her arms folded, staring at her. María gave up. Nevertheless, they dragged her to the ward for violent patients, subdued her with a hose spurting icy water, and injected turpentine into her legs. The swelling that resulted prevented her from walking, and María realized there was nothing in the world she would not do to escape that hell. The following week, when she was back in the dormitory, she tiptoed to the night matron's room and knocked at the door.

María's price, which she demanded in advance, was that the matron send a message to her husband. The matron agreed, on the condition that their dealings be kept an absolute secret. And she pointed an inexorable forefinger at her.

"If they ever find out, you die."

And so, on the following Saturday, Saturno the Magician drove to the asylum for women in the circus van, which he had prepared to celebrate María's return. The director himself received him in his office, which was as clean and well ordered as a battleship, and made an affectionate report on his wife's condition. No one had known where she came from, or how or when, since the first information regarding her arrival was the official admittance form he had dictated after interviewing her. An investigation begun that same day had proved inconclusive. In any event, what most intrigued the director was how Saturno had learned his wife's whereabouts. Saturno protected the matron.

"The insurance company told me," he said.

The director nodded, satisfied. "I don't know how insurance companies manage to find out everything," he said. He looked over the file lying on his ascetic's desk, and concluded:

"The only certainty is the seriousness of her condition."

He was prepared to authorize a visit with all the necessary precautions if Saturno the Magician would promise, for the good of his wife, to adhere without question to the rules of behavior that he would indicate. Above all with reference to how he treated her, in order to avoid a recurrence of the fits of rage that were becoming more and more frequent and dangerous.

"How strange," said Saturno. "She always was quick-tempered, but had a lot of self-control."

The doctor made a learned man's gesture. "There are behaviors that remain latent for many years, and then one day they erupt," he said. "All in all, it is fortunate she happened to come here, because we specialize in cases requiring a firm hand." Then he warned him about María's strange obsession with the telephone.

"Humor her," he said.

"Don't worry, Doctor," Saturno said with a cheerful air. "That's my specialty."

The visiting room, a combination of prison cell and confessional, was the former locutory of the convent. Saturno's entrance was not the explosion of joy they both might have expected. María stood in the middle of the room, next to a small table with two chairs and a vase empty of flowers. It was obvious she was ready to leave, with her lamentable strawberry-colored coat and a pair of disreputable shoes given to her out of charity. Herculina stood in a corner, almost invisible, her arms folded. María did not move when she saw her husband come in, and her face, still marked by the shattered window glass, showed no emotion. They exchanged routine kisses.

"How do you feel?" he asked her.

"Happy you're here at last, baby," she said. "This has been death."

They did not have time to sit down. Drowning in tears, María told him about the miseries of the cloister, the brutality of the matrons, the food not fit for dogs, the endless nights when terror kept her from closing her eyes.

"I don't even know how many days I've been here, or how many months or years, all I know is that each one has been worse than the last," and she sighed with all her soul. "I don't think I'll ever be the same."

"That's all over now," he said, caressing the recent scars on her face with his fingertips. "I'll come every Saturday. More often than that, if the director lets me. You'll see, everything will turn out just fine."

She fixed her terrified eyes on his. Saturno tried to use his performer's charm. He told her, in the puerile tone of all great lies, a sweetened version of the doctor's prognosis. "It means," he concluded, "that you still need a few more days to make a complete recovery." María understood the truth.

"For God's sake, baby," she said, stunned. "Don't tell me you think I'm crazy too!"

"The things you think of!" he said, trying to laugh. "But it really will be much better for everybody if you stay here a while. Under better conditions, of course."

"But I've already told you I only came to use the phone!" said María.

He did not know how to react to her dreadful obsession. He looked at Herculina. She took advantage of the opportunity to point at her wristwatch as a sign that it was time to end the visit. María intercepted the signal, glanced behind her, and saw Herculina tensing for an imminent attack. Then she clung to her husband's neck, screaming like a real madwoman. He freed himself with as much love as he could muster, and left her to the mercies of Herculina, who jumped her from behind. Without giving María time to react, she applied an arm-lock with her left hand, put her other iron arm around her throat, and shouted at Saturno the Magician:

"Leave!"

Saturno fled in terror.

But on the following Saturday, when he had recovered from the shock of the visit, he returned to the sanatorium with the cat, which he had dressed in an outfit identical to his: the red-and-yellow tights of the great Leotardo, a top hat, and a swirling cape that seemed made for flying. He drove the circus van into the courtyard of the cloister, and there he put on a prodigious show lasting almost three hours, which the inmates enjoyed from the balconies with discordant shouts and inopportune applause. They were all there except María, who not only refused to receive her husband but would not even watch him from the balconies. Saturno felt wounded to the quick.

"It is a typical reaction," the director consoled him. "It will pass."

But it never passed. After attempting many times to see María again, Saturno did all he could to have her accept a letter from him, but to no avail. She returned it four times, unopened and with no comments. Saturno gave up but continued leaving a supply of cigarettes at the porter's office without ever finding out if they reached María, until at last reality defeated him.

No one heard any more about him except that he married again and returned to his own country. Before leaving Barcelona he gave the half-starved cat to a casual girlfriend, who also promised to take cigarettes to María. But she disappeared too. Rosa Regás remembered seeing her in the Corte Inglés department store about twelve years ago, with the shaved head and orange robes of some Oriental sect, and very pregnant. She told Rosa she had taken cigarettes to María as often as she could, and settled some unforeseen emergencies for her, until one day she found only the ruins of the hospital, which had been demolished like a bad memory of those wretched times. María seemed very lucid on her last visit, a little overweight, and content with the peace of the cloister. That was the day she also brought María the cat, because she had spent all the money that Saturno had given her for its food.

APRIL 1978

The Ghosts of August

W E   R E A C H E D Arezzo a little before noon, and
spent more than two hours looking for the Renaissance
castle that the Venezuelan writer Miguel Otero Silva had
bought in that idyllic corner of the Tuscan countryside.
It was a burning, bustling Sunday in early August, and
it was not easy to find anyone who knew anything in the
streets teeming with tourists. After many useless attempts,
we went back to the car and left the city by a road lined
with cypresses but without any signs, and an old woman
tending geese told us with precision where the castle was
located. Before saying good-bye she asked us if we
planned to sleep there, and we replied that we were going only for lunch, which was our original intention.

"That's just as well," she said, "because the house is
haunted."

My wife and I, who do not believe in midday phantoms, laughed at her credulity. But our two sons, nine and seven years old, were overjoyed at the idea of meeting a ghost in the flesh.

Miguel Otero Silva, who was a splendid host and a refined gourmet as well as a good writer, had an unforgettable lunch waiting for us. Because we arrived late, we did not have time to see the inside of the castle before sitting down at the table, but there was nothing frightening about its external appearance, and any uneasiness was dissipated by our view of the entire city from the flower-covered terrace where we ate lunch. It was difficult to believe that so many men of lasting genius had been born on that hill crowded with houses with barely enough room for ninety thousand people. Miguel Otero Silva, however, said with his Caribbean humor that none of them was the most renowned native of Arezzo.

"The greatest of all," he declared, "was Ludovico."

Just like that, with no family names: Ludovico, the great patron of the arts and of war, who had built this castle of his affliction, and about whom Miguel spoke all during lunch. He told us of Ludovico's immense power, his troubled love, his dreadful death. He told us how it was that in a moment of heart's madness he stabbed his lady in the bed where they had just made love, turned his ferocious fighting dogs on himself, and was torn to pieces. He assured us, in all seriousness, that after midnight the ghost of Ludovico walked the dark of the house trying to find peace in his purgatory of love.

The castle really was immense and gloomy. But in the light of day, with a full stomach and a contented heart,

Miguel's tale seemed only another of the many diversions with which he entertained his guests. After our siesta we walked without foreboding through the eighty-two rooms that had undergone all kinds of alterations by a succession of owners. Miguel had renovated the entire first floor and built a modern bedroom with marble floors, a sauna, and exercise equipment, as well as the terrace covered with brilliant flowers where we had eaten lunch. The second story, the one most used over the centuries, consisted of characterless rooms with furnishings from different periods which had been abandoned to their fate. But on the top floor we saw a room, preserved intact, that time had forgotten to visit—the bedchamber of Ludovico.

The moment was magical. There stood the bed, its curtains embroidered in gold thread, the bedspread and its prodigies of passementerie still stiff with the dried blood of his sacrificed lover. There was the fireplace with its icy ashes and its last log turned to stone, the armoire with its weapons primed, and, in a gold frame, the oil portrait of the pensive knight, painted by some Florentine master who did not have the good fortune to survive his time. What affected me most, however, was the unexplainable scent of fresh strawberries that hung over the entire bedroom.

The days of summer are long and unhurried in Tuscany, and the horizon stays in its place until nine at night. When we finished walking through the castle it was after five, but Miguel insisted on taking us to see the frescoes by Piero della Francesca in the Church of San Francesco.

Then we lingered over coffee beneath the arbors on the square, and when we came back for our suitcases we found a meal waiting for us. And so we stayed for supper.

While we ate under a mauve sky with a single star, the boys took flashlights from the kitchen and set out to explore the darkness on the upper floors. From the table we could hear the gallop of wild horses on the stairs, the lamenting doors, the joyous shouts calling for Ludovico in the gloomy rooms. They were the ones who had the wicked idea of sleeping there. A delighted Miguel Otero Silva supported them, and we did not have the social courage to tell them no.

Contrary to what I had feared, we slept very well, my wife and I in a first-floor bedroom and the children in one adjoining ours. Both rooms had been modernized and there was nothing gloomy about them. As I waited for sleep I counted the twelve insomniac strokes of the pendulum clock in the drawing room, and I remembered the fearsome warning of the woman tending geese. But we were so tired that we soon fell into a dense, unbroken slumber, and I woke after seven to a splendid sun shining through the climbing vines at the window. Beside me my wife sailed the calm sea of the innocent. "What foolishness," I said to myself, "to still believe in ghosts in this day and age." Only then was I shaken by the scent of fresh strawberries, and I saw the fireplace with its cold ashes and its final log turned to stone, and the portrait of the melancholy knight in the gold frame looking at us over a distance of three centuries. For we were not in the first-floor bedroom where we had fallen asleep the night before, but in the bedchamber of Ludovico, under the canopy and the dusty curtains and the sheets soaked with still-warm blood of his accursed bed.

october 1980

Maria dos Prazeres

THE MAN FROM the undertaking establishment was so punctual that Maria dos Prazeres was still in her bathrobe, with her hair in curlers, and she just had time to put a red rose behind her ear to keep from looking as unattractive as she felt. She regretted her appearance even more when she opened the door and saw that he was not a mournful notary, as she supposed all death's merchants must be, but a timid young man wearing a checked jacket and a tie with birds in different colors. He had no overcoat, despite the unpredictable Barcelona spring and its oblique, wind-driven rain, which almost always made it less tolerable than the winter. Maria dos Prazeres, who had received so many men regardless of the hour, felt a rare embarrassment. She had just turned seventy-six and was convinced she would die before Christmas, but even so she was about to close the door and ask the funeral salesman to wait a moment while she dressed to receive him in the manner he deserved. Then it occurred to her that he would freeze on the dark landing, and she asked him in.

"Please excuse my awful appearance," she said, "but I've lived in Catalonia for over fifty years, and this is the first time anyone has ever come to an appointment on time."

She spoke perfect Catalan, with a somewhat archaic purity, although one could hear the music of her forgotten Portuguese. Despite her age and the metal curlers, she was still a slender, spirited mulatta, with wiry hair and pitiless yellow eyes, who had lost her compassion for men a long time ago. The salesman, half blinded by the light in the street, made no comment but wiped the soles of his shoes on the jute mat and kissed her hand with a bow.

"You're like the men in my day," said Maria dos Prazeres with a laugh sharp as hail. "Sit down."

Although he was new at the job, he knew enough about it not to expect this kind of festive welcome at eight o'clock in the morning, least of all from a merciless old lady who at first glance seemed a madwoman escaped from the Americas. And so he remained only a step away from the door, not knowing what to say, while Maria dos Prazeres pushed back the heavy plush drapes at the windows. The thin April light just reached the corners of the meticulous room, which looked more like an antique dealer's show window than a parlor. The objects in it were meant for daily use—there were not too many or too few—and each one seemed placed in its natural space with such sureness of taste that it would have been dif-

ficult to find a better-served house even in a city as old
and secret as Barcelona.

"Excuse me," he said. "I've come to the wrong door."

"I wish that were true," she said, "but death makes no
mistakes."

On the dining room table the salesman spread open a
diagram that had as many folds as a navigation chart, and
sections in different colors with numerous crosses and
figures in each color. Maria dos Prazeres saw that it was
the complete plan of the immense cemetery of Montjuich, and she remembered with an ancient horror the
graveyard in Manaus under the October rains, when tapirs
splashed among nameless tombs and adventurers' mauso-
leums with Florentine stained-glass windows. One morning, when she was a very little girl, the Amazon in flood
had become a sickening swamp, and in the courtyard
of her house she had seen the broken coffins floating
with pieces of rag and the hair of the dead coming through
the cracks. That memory was the reason she had chosen
the hill of Montjuich as her final resting place and not the
small San Gervasio cemetery, so much closer and more
familiar.

"I want a place that will never flood," she said.

"Well, here it is," said the salesman, indicating the
spot on the map with a collapsible pointer that he carried
in his pocket like a fountain pen. "No ocean in the world
can come up this high."

She studied the colored panels until she found the main
entrance and the three adjacent, identical, anonymous
graves where Buenaventura Durruti, killed in the Civil
War, and two other anarchist leaders lay buried. Every

night someone wrote their names on the blank stones. Wrote them with pencil, with paint, with charcoal, with eyebrow pencil or nail polish, and every morning the guards wiped them clean so that no one would know who lay under which mute stone. Maria dos Prazeres had attended Durruti's funeral, the saddest and most tumultuous ever held in Barcelona, and she wanted to rest in a grave near his. But none was available, and she resigned herself to what was possible. "On the condition," she said, "that you don't decide to stack me in one of those five-year compartments as if it were the post office." Then, remembering the essential requirement, she concluded: "And above all, I have to be buried lying down." For in response to the much-publicized promotion of prepaid graves, a rumor was circulating that they were making vertical burials to save space. With the precision of someone who had memorized and repeated a speech many times, the salesman explained that the story was a wicked lie created by traditional undertaking establishments to discredit the unprecedented sale of graves on the installment plan. As he spoke, there were three discreet little taps at the door, and he paused with some uncertainty, but Maria dos Prazeres indicated that he should go on. "Don't worry," she said in a very quiet voice. "It's Noi."

The salesman took up where he had left off, and Maria dos Prazeres felt satisfied with his explanation. Still, before opening the door she wanted to make a final synthesis of a thought that had been ripening in her heart, down to its most intimate details, over the many years since the legendary flood in Manaus. "What I mean," she said, "is that I am looking for a place where I can lie down in the

earth with no risk of floods and, if possible, in the shade
of the trees in summer, and where I won't be pulled out
after a certain period of time and thrown away in the
trash."

She opened the front door and in walked a small dog
drenched with rain, whose dissolute appearance had nothing to do with the rest of the house. He was returning
from his morning walk through the neighborhood, and
as he came in he suffered a sudden fit of tumultuous ex-
citement. He jumped on the table, barking in a crazed
way and almost ruining the map of the cemetery with
his muddy paws. A single glance from his owner was
enough to restrain his impetuosity. "Noi!" she said without raising her voice. "*Baixa d'aci!*"

The animal shrank back, looked at her in consternation, and two bright tears rolled down his muzzle. Then
Maria dos Prazeres turned her attention again to the salesman, and found him mystified.

"*Collons!*" he exclaimed. "He cried!"

"It's just that he's upset at finding someone here at this
hour," Maria dos Prazeres apologized in a low voice. "In
general, when he comes into the house he shows more care
than men do. Except for you, as I've already seen."

"But he cried, damn it!" the salesman repeated, then
realized his breach of good manners and begged her par-
don with a blush. "Excuse me, but I've never seen anything like that, even in the movies."

"All dogs can do it if you train them," she said. "But
instead the owners spend their whole lives teaching them
habits that make them miserable, like eating from plates
or doing their business on schedule and in the same place.

And yet they don't teach them the natural things they enjoy, like laughing and crying. Where were we?"

They were almost finished. Maria dos Prazeres also had to resign herself to summers without trees, because the only ones in the cemetery had their shade reserved for dignitaries of the regime. On the other hand, the conditions and formulas in the contract were irrelevant, because she wanted to take advantage of the discount she would receive for paying cash in advance.

It was not until they had finished and the salesman was putting the papers back into his briefcase that he looked at the room with more observant eyes, and he shivered in the magic air of its beauty. He looked at Maria dos Prazeres again, as if for the first time.

"May I ask you an indiscreet question?" he said.

She walked with him toward the door.

"Of course," she said. "As long as it's not my age."

"I'm in the habit of guessing people's occupations from the things in their houses, and the truth is that here I can't tell," he said. "What do you do?"

Overcome with laughter, Maria dos Prazeres answered: "I'm a whore, my boy. Or don't I look like one anymore?"

The salesman turned red. "I'm sorry."

"I should be sorrier," she said, taking him by the arm to keep him from crashing into the door. "And be careful! Don't crack your skull before you've given me a proper burial."

As soon as she closed the door, she picked up the little dog and began to pet him, and with her beautiful African voice she joined in the children's songs that could be heard just then coming from the nursery school next door. Three months ago it had been revealed to her in a dream that she would die, and from that time on she had felt closer than ever to this child of her solitude. She had anticipated the posthumous distribution of her belongings and the disposition of her body with so much care that she could have died at that moment without inconveniencing anyone. She had retired of her own volition, with a fortune she had accumulated stone by stone but without too many bitter sacrifices, and she had chosen as her final home the very ancient and noble town of Gracia, which had already been swallowed up by the expanding city. She had bought the dilapidated second-floor apartment, with its perpetual smell of smoked herring and its walls eaten away by saltpeter but still showing all the bullet holes of some inglorious battle. There was no porter, and even though all the apartments were occupied, some steps were missing on the damp, dark stairways. Maria dos Prazeres had the bathroom and kitchen remodeled, covered the walls with bright fabrics, put beveled glass in the windows, and hung velvet drapes. Then she brought in the exquisite furnishings—the useful and decorative objects and the chests of silks and brocades, which the Fascists had stolen from residences abandoned by the Republicans in the stampede of defeat, and which for many years she had been buying one by one for bargain prices at secret auctions. The only remaining link to her past was her friendship with the Count of Cardona, who continued visiting her on the last Friday of every month to have supper with her and make languid, after-dinner love. But even that friendship from her youth was kept hidden, for the Count parked the automobile that bore his coat of arms at a more than discreet distance, and he walked to her second floor in the shadows, as much to protect her honor as his own. Maria dos Prazeres knew no one in the building except the people in the apartment opposite hers, where a very young couple with a nine-year-old daughter had moved in not long ago. It seemed incredible to her, but in fact she had never met anyone else on the stairs.

And yet the distribution of her legacy revealed that she was more rooted than she had supposed in that community of unreconstructed Catalonians whose national honor was founded on the virtue of decent modesty. She had left even the most insignificant trinkets to the people closest to her heart, who were the people closest to her house. When it was over she did not feel very convinced that she had been fair, but she was certain she had not forgotten anyone who did not deserve it. She had prepared the bequests with so much rigor that the notary on the Calle del Árbol, who flattered himself on having seen everything, could not believe his eyes when he saw her dictating to his clerks from memory, in medieval Catalan, the detailed list of her possessions, along with the exact name of each item, and the complete list of beneficiaries with their professions and addresses and the place each held in her heart.

After the visit of the funeral salesman, she became one of the countless Sunday visitors to the cemetery. Like her graveyard neighbors, she planted year-round flowers in the urns, watered the new grass and trimmed it with pruning shears until it resembled the carpets in the mayor's office, and became so familiar with the spot that in the end she could not understand why it had seemed so desolate to her in the beginning.

On her first visit, her heart had skipped a beat when she saw the three nameless graves near the gate, but she did not even stop to look at them, because the vigilant watchman was a few steps away from her. But on the third Sunday she took advantage of a moment's carelessness to fulfill one of her great dreams, and with her lipstick she wrote on the first, rain-washed stone: *Durruti*. From then on, whenever she could she did it again, sometimes on one gravestone, or on two or on all three, and always with a firm pulse and a heart stirred by nostalgia.

One Sunday, in late September, she witnessed her first burial on the hill. Three weeks later, on a cold, windy afternoon, they buried a young bride in the grave next to hers. By the end of the year, seven plots were occupied, but the short-lived winter passed with no ill effects on Maria dos Prazeres. She suffered no indisposition, and as the weather grew warmer and the torrential sound of life poured in through the open windows, she felt more determined to survive the enigmas of her dreams. On his return, the Count of Cardona, who spent the hottest months in the mountains, found her even more attractive than she had been in the uncommon youthfulness of her fiftieth year.

After many frustrated attempts, Maria dos Prazeres succeeded in having Noi pick out her grave on the massive hill of identical graves. Then she devoted herself to teaching him to cry over the empty tomb so that he would be in the habit of doing so after her death. She walked with him several times from her house to the cemetery, pointing out landmarks to help him memorize the Ramblas bus route, until she felt that he was skilled enough to be sent on his own.

On the Sunday of the final test, at three o'clock in the afternoon, she took off his spring vest, in part because summer was in the air and in part to make him less conspicuous, and turned him loose. She saw him go down the shady side of the street at a quick trot, his little rump tight and sad beneath his jubilant tail, and it was all she could do not to cry—for herself, for him, for so many and such bitter years of shared illusions—until she saw him turn the corner at the Calle Mayor and head for the sea. Fifteen minutes later she took the Ramblas bus at the nearby Plaza de Lesseps, trying to see him through the window without being seen, and in fact she did see him, distant and serious among the Sunday flocks of children, waiting for the traffic light to change at the Paseo de Gracia.

"My God," she sighed. "He looks so alone."

She had to wait for him for almost two hours under the brutal Montjuich sun. She greeted several of the bereaved from other, less memorable Sundays, although she almost did not recognize them, because so much time had gone by since she had first seen them that they no longer wore mourning or cried, and they put flowers on the graves without thinking about their dead. A short while later, when they had all left, she heard a mournful bellow that startled the sea gulls, and on the immense sea she saw a white ocean liner flying the Brazilian flag, and with all her heart she wished that it were bringing her a letter from someone who would have died for her in Pernambuco prison. A little after five o'clock, twelve minutes ahead of schedule, Noi appeared on the hill, slavering with fatigue and the heat, but with the air of a triumphant child. At that moment Maria dos Prazeres overcame the terror of not having anyone to cry at her grave.

The following autumn was when she began to detect ominous signs that she could not decipher but that made her heart heavier. She drank coffee again under the golden acacias on the Plaza del Reloj, wearing her coat with the foxtail collar and the hat decorated with artificial flowers, which was so old it had become fashionable again. Her intuition grew more acute. Trying to understand her own disquiet, she scrutinized the chatter of the women selling birds on the Ramblas, the gossip of the men at the book-stalls—who for the first time in many years were not talking about soccer—the deep silences of the crippled war veterans tossing bread crumbs to the pigeons, and every-where she found unmistakable signs of death. At Christ-mas, colored lights were strung between the acacias, and music and happy voices were heard from the balconies, and a crowd of tourists invaded the sidewalk cafés, but in the midst of all the festivities one could feel the same repressed tension that preceded the days when the anar-chists had taken over the streets. Maria dos Prazeres, who had lived through that time of great passions, could not control her uneasiness, and for the first time she was awak-ened from her sleep by the clawing of fear. One night, outside her window, state security agents shot and killed a student who had scrawled *Visca Catalunya lliure* on the wall.

"My God," she said to herself in terror, "it's as if everything were dying with me!"

She had known this kind of disquiet only when she was a very little girl in Manaus, at the moment before dawn, when the innumerable sounds of night stopped all at once, the waters paused, time hesitated, and the Amazon jungle sank into an abysmal silence that was like the silence of death. In the midst of that irresistible tension, on the last Friday of April, as always, the Count of Cardona came to her house for supper.

The visit had turned into a ritual. The punctual Count would arrive between seven and nine at night with a bottle of local champagne, wrapped in the afternoon paper to make it less noticeable, and a box of filled truffles. Maria dos Prazeres prepared cannelloni au gratin and a young chicken au jus—the favorite dishes from the halcyon days of fine old Catalonian families—and a bowl filled with fruits of the season. While she cooked, the Count listened to selections from historic performances of Italian operas on the phonograph, taking slow sips from a glass of port that lasted until the records were over.

After the unhurried supper and conversation, they made sedentary love from memory, which left both of them with a taste of disaster. Before he left, always restless at the approach of midnight, the Count put twenty-five pesetas under the ashtray in the bedroom. That was Maria dos Prazeres's price when he first met her in a transient hotel on the Paralelo, and it was all that the rust of time had left intact.

Neither of them had ever wondered what their friendship was based on. Maria dos Prazeres owed him some simple favors. He gave her helpful advice on managing her savings; he had taught her to recognize the true value of her relics, and how to keep them so that no one would discover they were stolen goods. But above all he was the one who showed her the road to a decent old age in the Gracia district, when they said in the brothel where she had spent her life that she was too old for modern tastes, and wanted to send her to a house for retired ladies of the night who taught boys how to make love for a fee of five pesetas. She had told the Count that her mother sold her in the port of Manaus when she was fourteen years old, and that the first mate of a Turkish ship used her without mercy during the Atlantic crossing, and then abandoned her, with no money, no language, and no name, in the light-filled swamp of the Paralelo. They were both conscious of having so little in common that they never felt more alone than when they were together, but neither one had dared to spoil the pleasures of habit. It took a national upheaval for them to realize, both at the same time, how much they had hated each other, and with how much tenderness, for so many years.

It was a sudden conflagration. The Count of Cardona was listening to the love duet from *La Bohème*, sung by Licia Albanese and Beniamino Gigli, when he happened to hear a news bulletin on the radio that Maria dos Prazeres was listening to in the kitchen. He tiptoed over and listened as well. General Francisco Franco, eternal dictator of Spain, had assumed responsibility for deciding the fate of three Basque separatists who had just been condemned to death. The Count breathed a sigh of relief.

"Then they'll be shot without fail," he said, "because the Caudillo is a just man."

Maria dos Prazeres stared at him with the burning eyes of a royal cobra and saw the passionless pupils behind gold-rimmed spectacles, the ravening teeth, the hybrid hands of an animal accustomed to dampness and dark. Saw him just as he was.

"Well, you'd better pray he doesn't," she said, "because if they shoot even one of them I'll poison your soup."

The Count was flabbergasted. "Why would you do that?"

"Because I'm a just whore, too."

The Count of Cardona never returned, and Maria dos Prazeres was certain that the final cycle of her life had come to an end. Until a little while before, in fact, she had felt indignant when anyone offered her a seat on the bus, or tried to help her across the street or take her arm to go up stairs, but she came not only to allow such things but even to desire them as a hateful necessity. That was when she ordered an anarchist's tombstone, with no name or dates, and began to sleep with the door unlocked so that Noi could get out with the news if she died in her sleep.

One Sunday, as she was coming home from the cemetery, she met the little girl from the apartment across the

landing. She walked with her for several blocks, talking
about everything with a grandmother's innocence while
she watched her and Noi playing like old friends. On the
Plaza del Diamante, just as she had planned, she offered
to buy her ice cream. "Do you like dogs?" she asked.

"I love them," said the girl.

Then Maria dos Prazeres made the proposal that she
had been preparing for so long. "If anything ever happens to me, I want you to take Noi," she said. "On the
condition that you let him loose on Sundays and not think
any more about it. He'll know what to do."

The girl was delighted. And Maria dos Prazeres returned home with the joy of having lived a dream that
had ripened for years in her heart. But it was not because
of the weariness of old age or the belated arrival of death
that the dream was not realized. It was not even her decision. Life made it for her one icy November afternoon
when a sudden storm broke as she was leaving the cemetery. She had written the names on the three tomb-
stones and was walking down to the bus station when the
downpour soaked her to the skin. She just had time to
take shelter in a doorway of a deserted district that seemed
to belong to another city, with dilapidated warehouses
and dusty factories, and enormous trailer trucks that
made the awful noise of the storm even more frightening.
As she tried to warm the drenched dog with her body,
Maria dos Prazeres saw the crowded buses pass by, she
saw empty taxis pass by with their flags up, but no one
paid attention to her distress signals. Then, when even a
miracle seemed impossible, a sumptuous, almost noiseless

car the color of dusky steel passed by along the flooded street, made a sudden stop at the corner, and came back in reverse to where she stood. The windows lowered as if by magic, and the driver offered her a lift.

"I'm going quite a distance," said Maria dos Prazeres with sincerity. "But you would do me a great favor if you could take me part of the way."

"Tell me where you're going," he insisted.

"To Gracia," she said.

The door opened without his touching it.

"It's on my way," he said. "Get in."

The interior smelled of refrigerated medicine, and once she was inside, the rain became an unreal mishap, the city changed color, and she felt she was in a strange, happy world where everything was arranged ahead of time. The driver made his way through the disorder of the traffic with a fluidity that had a touch of magic. Maria dos Prazeres felt intimidated not only by her own misery but by that of the pitiful little dog asleep in her lap.

"This is an ocean liner," she said, because she felt she had to say something appropriate. "I've never seen anything like it, not even in my dreams."

"Really, the only thing wrong with it is that it doesn't belong to me," he said in an awkward Catalan, and after a pause he added in Castilian, "What I earn in a lifetime wouldn't be enough to buy it."

"I can imagine," she sighed.

Out of the corner of her eye she examined him in the

green light of the dashboard, and she saw that he was little more than an adolescent, with short curly hair and the profile of a Roman bronze. She thought that he was not handsome but had a distinctive kind of charm, that his worn, cheap leather jacket was very becoming, and that his mother must feel very happy when she heard him walk in the door. Only his laborer's hands made it possible to believe that he was not the owner of the car.

They did not speak again for the rest of the trip, but Maria dos Prazeres also sensed that he examined her several times out of the corner of his eye, and once again she regretted still being alive at her age. She felt ugly and pitiful, with the housemaid's shawl she had thrown over her head when the rain began, and the deplorable autumn coat she had not thought to change because she was thinking about death.

When they reached the Gracia district it was beginning to clear, night had fallen, and the streetlights were on. Maria dos Prazeres told the driver to let her off at a nearby corner, but he insisted on taking her to her front door, and he not only did that but pulled up on the sidewalk so that she could get out of the car without getting wet. She released the dog, attempted to climb out with as much dignity as her body would allow, and when she turned to thank him she met a male stare that took her breath away. She endured it for a moment, not understanding very well who was waiting for what, or from whom, and then he asked in a determined voice: "Shall I come up?"

Maria dos Prazeres felt humiliated. "I am very grateful for your kindness in bringing me here," she said, "but I will not permit you to make fun of me."

"I have no reason to make fun of anybody," he said with absolute seriousness, in Castilian. "Least of all a woman like you."

Maria dos Prazeres had known many men like him, had saved many men bolder than he from suicide, but never in her long life had she been so afraid to make up her mind. She heard him repeat without the slightest change in his voice: "Shall I come up?"

She walked away without closing the car door, and answered in Castilian to be sure he understood. "Do whatever you want."

She walked into the lobby, dim in the oblique light from the street, and began to climb the first flight of stairs with trembling knees, choked by a fear she would have thought possible only at the moment of death. When she stopped outside the door on the second floor, shaking with desperation to find her keys in her bag, she heard two car doors slam, one after the other, in the street. Noi, who had preceded her, tried to bark. "Be quiet," she ordered in an agonized whisper. Then she heard the first steps on the loose risers of the stairway and was afraid her heart would burst. In a fraction of a second she made a thorough reexamination of the premonitory dream that had changed her life for the past three years, and she saw the error of her interpretation.

"My God," she said to herself in astonishment. "So it wasn't death!"

Maria dos Prazeres

At last she found the lock, listening to the measured footsteps in the dark, listening to the heightened breathing of someone who approached in the dark with as much astonishment as she felt, and then she knew it had been worth waiting so many years, worth so much suffering in the dark, if only to live that moment.

MAY 1979

Seventeen Poisoned
Englishmen

THE FIRST THING Señora Prudencia Linero noticed when she reached the port of Naples was that it
had the same smell as the port of Riohacha. She did not
tell anyone, of course, since no one would have understood on that senile ocean liner filled to overflowing with
Italians from Buenos Aires who were returning to their
native land for the first time since the war, but in any
case, at the age of seventy-two, and at a distance of eighteen days of heavy seas from her people and her home,
she felt less alone, less frightened and remote.

The lights on land had been visible since daybreak.
The passengers got up earlier than usual, wearing new
clothes, their hearts heavy with the uncertainties of putting ashore, so that the last Sunday on board seemed to be
the only genuine one of the entire voyage. Señora Pru

dencia Linero was one of the very few who attended Mass. In contrast to the clothes she had worn before, when she walked around the ship dressed in partial mourning, today she had on a tunic of coarse brown burlap tied with the cord of Saint Francis, and rough leather sandals that did not resemble a pilgrim's only because they were too new. It was an advance payment: She had promised God that she would wear the full-length habit for the rest of her life if He blessed her with a trip to Rome to see the Supreme Pontiff, and she already considered the blessing granted. When Mass was over she lit a candle to the Holy Spirit in gratitude for the infusion of courage that had allowed her to endure the Caribbean storms, and she said a prayer for each of her nine children and fourteen grand-children who at that very moment were dreaming about her on a windy night in Riohacha.

When she went up on deck after breakfast, life on the ship had changed. Luggage was piled in the ballroom, along with all kinds of tourist trinkets the Italians had bought at the magic markets of the Antilles, and on the saloon bar there was a macaque from Pernambuco in a wrought-iron cage. It was a brilliant morning in early August. One of those exemplary postwar summer Sun-days when the light was like a daily revelation, and the enormous ship inched along, with an invalid's labored breathing, through a transparent stillwater. The gloomy fortress of the Dukes of Anjou was just beginning to loom on the horizon, but the passengers who had come on deck thought they recognized familiar places, and they pointed at them without quite seeing them, shouting with joy in their southern dialects. To her surprise, Señora

Prudencia Linero, who had made so many dear old friends on board, who had watched children while their parents danced, and even sewn a button on the first officer's tunic, found them all distant and changed. The social spirit and human warmth that permitted her to survive her first homesickness in the stifling heat of the tropics had disappeared. The eternal loves of the high seas ended when the port came into view. Señora Prudencia Linero, who was not familiar with the voluble nature of Italians, thought the problem lay not in the hearts of others but in her own, since she was the only one going in a crowd that was returning. Every voyage must be like this, she thought, suffering for the first time in her life the sharp pain of being a foreigner, while she leaned on the railing and contemplated the vestiges of so many extinct worlds in the depths of the water. All at once a very beautiful girl standing beside her startled her with a scream of horror.

"*Mamma mia*," she cried, pointing down. "Look over there."

It was a drowned man. Señora Prudencia Linero saw him drifting faceup, a mature, bald man of rare natural distinction, with open, joyful eyes the color of the sky at dawn. He wore full evening dress with a brocade vest, patent-leather shoes, and a fresh gardenia in his lapel. In his right hand he held a little square package wrapped in gift paper, and his pale iron fingers clutched at the bow, which was all he had found to hold on to at the moment of his death.

"He must have fallen from a wedding party," said

one of the ship's officers. "It happens pretty often in these waters during the summer."

It was a momentary vision, because just then they were entering the bay, and other, less mournful subjects distracted the attention of the passengers. But Señora Prudencia Linero continued to think about the drowned man, the poor drowned man, whose long-tailed jacket rippled in their wake.

As soon as the ship sailed into the harbor, a decrepit tugboat came out to meet it and lead it by the nose through the wreckage of countless military craft destroyed during the war. The water was turning into oil as the ship made its way past the rusting wrecks, and the heat became even fiercer than in Riohacha at two in the afternoon. On the other side of the narrow channel, the city, brilliant in the eleven-o'clock sun, came into view with all its chimerical palaces and ancient, painted hovels crowded together on the hills. Just then an unbearable stench rose from the disturbed bottom, which Señora Prudencia Linero recognized from the courtyard of her house as the foul breath of rotting crabs.

While this maneuver took place, the passengers, with great displays of joy, recognized their relatives in the tumultuous crowd on the pier. Most of them were autumnal matrons with dazzling bosoms who suffocated in their mourning clothes and had the most beautiful and numerous children in the world, and small, diligent husbands, the immortal kind who read the newspaper after their wives and dress like stern notaries despite the heat.

In the midst of that carnival confusion, a very old man

wearing a beggar's overcoat and an inconsolable expression pulled a profusion of tiny chicks from his pockets with both hands. In an instant they covered the entire pier, crazed and cheeping, and it was only because they were magic that many survived and kept running after being stepped on by the crowd that was oblivious to the miracle. The wizard had placed his hat upside down on the ground, but nobody at the railing tossed him even one charitable coin.

Fascinated by the wondrous spectacle that seemed to be presented in her honor, for only she appreciated it, Señora Prudencia Linero was not aware of the exact moment when the gangplank was lowered and a human avalanche invaded the ship with the howling momentum of a pirate attack. Dazed by the wild jubilation and the rancid-onion smell of so many families in summer, shoved by the gangs of porters who came to blows over the baggage, she felt threatened by the same inglorious death that menaced the little chicks on the pier. That was when she sat down on her wooden trunk with its painted tin corners and remained there undaunted, intoning a vicious circle of prayers against temptation and danger in the lands of infidels. The first officer found her when the cataclysm had passed and she was the only one left in the abandoned ballroom.

"Nobody's supposed to be here now," the officer told her with a certain amiability. "Can I help you with something?"

"I have to wait for the consul," she said.

That was true. Two days before she sailed, her oldest son had sent a telegram to his friend the consul in Naples, asking him to meet his mother at the port and help her through the procedures for continuing on to Rome. He had told him the name of the ship and the time of its arrival, and that he would recognize her because she would be wearing the habit of Saint Francis when she came ashore. She was so uncompromising about these arrangements that the first officer allowed her to wait a little longer, although soon it would be time for the crew's lunch, and they had already put the chairs on the tables and were washing down the decks with buckets of water. They had to move her trunk several times in order not to wet it, but she changed places without changing expression, without interrupting her prayers, until they took her out of the recreation rooms and left her sitting in the full sun among the lifeboats. That was where the first officer found her again a little before two, drowning in sweat inside her penitent's garb, saying the Rosary with no expectations because she was terrified and sad and it was all she could do not to cry.

"It's useless for you to keep praying," said the officer, without his former amiability. "Even God goes on vacation in August."

He explained that at this time of year half of Italy was at the beach, above all on Sundays. In all likelihood the consul was not on vacation, given the nature of his responsibilities, but it was certain he would not open the office until Monday. The only reasonable thing was to go to a hotel, get a good night's sleep, and telephone the consulate the next day; no doubt the number was in the phone book. Señora Prudencia Linero had no choice but to accept his judgment, and the officer helped her through the procedures for immigration and customs and changing money, and put her in a taxi, with vague instructions that she be taken to a decent hotel. ╱

The decrepit taxi, with its traces of a funeral carriage, lurched down the deserted streets. For a moment Señora Prudencia Linero thought she and the driver were the only living creatures in a city of ghosts that hung from clotheslines in the middle of the street, but she also thought that a man who talked so much, and with so much passion, could not have time to harm a poor solitary woman who had risked the dangers of the ocean to see the Pope.

At the end of the labyrinth of streets she saw the sea again. The taxi continued to lurch along a burning, deserted beach where there were numerous small hotels painted in bright colors. It did not stop at any of these but drove straight to the least gaudy one, which was situated in a public garden with large palm trees and green benches. The driver placed the trunk on the shaded sidewalk, and when he saw Señora Prudencia Linero's uncertainty, he assured her that this was the most decent hotel in Naples.

A handsome, kindhearted porter hoisted the trunk on his shoulder and took charge of her. He led her to the metal grillwork elevator that had been improvised in the stairwell, and with alarming determination began to sing a Puccini aria at the top of his voice. It was a venerable building, with a different hotel on each of its nine renovated floors. All at once, in a kind of hallucination, Señora Prudencia Linero felt that she was in a chicken cage rising slowly through the center of an echoing marble staircase, catching glimpses of people in their houses with their most intimate misgivings, with their torn underwear and acidic belches. On the third floor the elevator jolted to a halt, and then the porter stopped singing, opened the sliding rhomboids of the door, and with a gallant bow indicated to Señora Prudencia Linero that she was in her house.

In the foyer she saw a languid adolescent behind a wooden counter with insets of colored glass and shade plants in copper pots. She liked him at once because he had the same angelic ringlets as her youngest grandson. She liked the name of the hotel, with its letters engraved on a bronze plaque, she liked the odor of carbolic acid, she liked the hanging ferns, the silence, the golden fleurs-de-lis on the wallpaper. Then she stepped out of the elevator, and her heart sank. A group of English tourists wearing shorts and beach sandals were dozing in a long row of easy chairs. There were seventeen of them, seated in symmetrical order, as if they were only one man repeated many times in a hall of mirrors. Señora Prudencia Linero took them in at a single glance without distinguishing one from the other, and all she could see was the long row of pink knees that looked like slabs of pork hanging from hooks in a butcher shop. She did not take another step toward the counter, but retreated in consternation into the elevator.

"Let's go to another floor," she said.

"This is the only one that has a dining room, Signora," said the porter.

"It doesn't matter," she said.

The porter made a gesture of consent, closed the elevator, and sang the remaining portion of the song until they came to the hotel on the fifth floor. Everything seemed less rigorous here, the owner was a springlike matron who spoke fluent Spanish, and no one was taking a siesta in the easy chairs in the foyer. There was in fact no dining room, but the hotel had arranged with a nearby restaurant to serve the guests at a reduced price. And so Señora Prudencia Linero decided yes, she would stay for one night, persuaded as much by the owner's eloquence and amiability as by her relief that not a single Englishman with pink knees was sleeping in the foyer.

At three in the afternoon the blinds in her room were closed, and the half-shadow preserved the cool silence of a hidden grove, and it was a good place to cry. As soon as she was alone, Señora Prudencia Linero bolted both locks, and for the first time since the morning she urinated, in a thin, hesitant stream that allowed her to recover the identity she had lost during the journey. Then she removed her sandals and the cord around her waist, and lay down on her left side on the double bed that was too wide and too lonely for her alone, and released the other flood of long-overdue tears.

Not only was this the first time she had left Riohacha, but it was one of the few times she had left her house after her children married and moved away, and she was alone with two barefoot Indian women to care for the soulless body of her husband. Half her life had been spent in the bedroom facing the ruins of the only man she ever loved, who for almost thirty years had been in a coma, lying on a goatskin mattress in the bed of their youthful lovemaking.

During the previous October, the invalid had opened his eyes in a sudden flash of lucidity, recognized his family, and asked them to send for a photographer. They brought in the old man from the park with the enormous bellows and black-sleeve camera and the magnesium plate for taking pictures in the home. The sick man himself arranged the photographs. "One for Prudencia, for the love and happiness she gave me in life," he said. This was taken with the first magnesium flash. "Now another two for my darling daughters, Prudencita and Natalia," he said. These were taken. "Another two for my sons, whose affection and good judgment make them examples to the family," he said. And so on until the photographer ran out of paper and had to go home for a new supply. At four o'clock, when the magnesium smoke and the tumultuous crowd of relatives, friends, and acquaintances who flocked to receive their copies of the portrait made the air in the bedroom unbreathable, the invalid began to lose consciousness in his bed, and he waved good-bye to everyone as if he were erasing himself from the world at the railing of a ship.

His death was not the relief for the widow that everyone had hoped for. On the contrary, she was so grief-stricken that her children gathered to ask what they could do to comfort her, and she replied that all she wanted was to go to Rome to meet the Pope.

"I'll go alone and wear the habit of Saint Francis," she informed them. "I've made a vow."

The only gratification remaining from those years of vigil was the pleasure of crying. On the ship, when she had to share her cabin with two Clarissine sisters who went ashore at Marseilles, she would linger in the bathroom to cry unseen. As a result the hotel room in Naples was the only suitable place she had found since leaving Riohacha where she could cry to her heart's content. And she would have cried until the following day, when the train left for Rome, if the owner had not knocked at her door at seven to say that if she did not go to the restaurant soon she would have nothing to eat.

The porter accompanied her. A cool breeze had begun to blow in from the sea, and there were still some bathers on the beach under the pale seven-o'clock sun. Señora Prudencia Linero followed the porter along a difficult terrain of steep, narrow streets that were just beginning to wake from their Sunday siesta, and then found herself in a shaded arbor where the tables were covered with red-checkered cloths and jars served as vases for paper flowers. At that early hour her only fellow diners were the waiters and waitresses and a very poor priest eating bread and onions at a back table. When she went in she felt everyone's eyes on her brown habit, but this did not affect her, for she knew that ridicule was part of her penance. The waitress, on the other hand, roused a spark of pity in her, because she was blonde and beautiful and spoke as if she were singing, and Señora Prudencia Linero thought that things must be very bad in Italy after the war if a girl like her had to wait on tables in a restaurant. But she felt at ease in the flowering arbor, and the aroma of stew with bay leaf from the kitchen awakened the hunger that had been deferred by the anxieties of the day. For the first time in a long while she had no desire to cry.

And yet she could not eat as she wished, in part because

it was difficult to communicate with the blonde waitress, even though she was kind and patient, and in part because some little songbirds, the kind kept in cages in the houses of Riohacha, were the only meat available. The priest who was eating in the corner, and later acted as interpreter, tried to make her understand that the emergencies of war had not ended in Europe, and the fact that at least there were little woodland birds to eat ought to be viewed as a miracle. But she pushed them away.

"For me," she said, "it would be like eating one of my children."

And so she had to settle for some vermicelli soup, a plate of squash boiled with a few shreds of rancid bacon, and a piece of bread as hard as marble. While she was eating, the priest approached her table to ask in the name of charity that she buy him a cup of coffee, and he sat down with her. He was from Yugoslavia but had been a missionary in Bolivia, and spoke an awkward, expressive Spanish. To Señora Prudencia Linero he seemed an ordinary man with no vestige of God's indulgence, and she observed that he had disgraceful hands with broken, dirty nails, and an onion breath so persistent it seemed more like a character trait. But he was in the service of God, after all, and it was a pleasure as well, when she was so far from home, to meet someone she could talk to.

They conversed at their leisure, oblivious to the heavy barnyard noise that began to surround them as more people sat at the other tables. Señora Prudencia Linero already had a definitive opinion of Italy: She did not like it. And not because the men were somewhat improper, which was saying a great deal, or because they ate song-

birds, which was going too far, but because they were in
the wicked habit of leaving drowned men to drift in the
water.

The priest, who had ordered a *grappa* at her expense
along with the coffee, tried to make her see the super-
ficiality of her opinion. For during the war they had
established a very efficient service for rescuing, identifying, and burying in holy ground the many drowning
victims found floating in the Bay of Naples.

"Centuries ago," the priest concluded, "the Italians
learned that there is only one life, and they try to live it
the best they can. This has made them calculating and
talkative, but it has also cured them of cruelty."

"They didn't even stop the ship," she said.

"What they do is radio the port authorities," said the
priest. "By now they've picked him up and buried him
in the name of God."

The discussion changed both their moods. Señora Prudencia Linero had finished eating, and only then did she
realize that all the tables were occupied. At the ones close
by, almost naked tourists sat eating in silence, among them
a few couples who kissed and did not eat. At the tables
in the rear, near the bar, neighborhood people played at
dice and drank a colorless wine. Señora Prudencia Linero
understood that she had only one reason for being in that
unsavory country.

"Do you think it will be very difficult to see the Pope?"
she asked.

The priest replied that nothing was easier in the summer. The Pope was on vacation in Castel Gandolfo, and
on Wednesday afternoons he held a public audience for

pilgrims from all over the world. The entrance fee was very cheap: twenty lire.

"And how much does he charge to hear a person's confession?" she asked.

"The Holy Father does not hear confessions," said the priest, somewhat scandalized, "except for those of kings, of course."

"I don't see why he would refuse that favor to a poor woman who's come so far," she said.

"And some kings, even though they're kings, have died waiting," said the priest. "But tell me: Yours must be an awful sin if you made such a journey all alone just to confess to the Holy Father."

Señora Prudencia Linero thought for a moment, and the priest saw her smile for the first time.

"Mother of God!" she said. "I'd be satisfied just to see him." And she added, with a sigh that seemed to come from her soul: "It's been my lifelong dream!"

The truth was that she still felt frightened and sad, and all she wanted was to leave the restaurant, as well as Italy, without delay. The priest must have thought he had gotten all he could from the deluded woman, and so he wished her good luck and went to another table to ask in the name of charity that they buy him a cup of coffee.

When she walked out of the restaurant, Señora Prudencia Linero found a changed city. She was surprised by the sunlight at nine o'clock, and frightened by the raucous throng that had invaded the streets to find relief in the evening breeze. The backfiring of so many crazed Vespas made life impossible. Driven by bare-chested men whose beautiful women sat behind them, hugging them around the waist, they moved in fits and starts, weaving in and out among hanging pigs and tables covered with melons.

It was a carnival atmosphere, but it seemed a catastrophe to Señora Prudencia Linero. She lost her way, and all at once found herself in an infelicitous street where taciturn women sat in the doorways of identical houses whose blinking red lights made her shiver with terror. A well-dressed man wearing a heavy gold ring and a diamond in his tie followed her for several blocks saying something in Italian, and then in English and French. When he received no reply, he showed her a postcard from a pack he took out of his pocket, and one glance was all she needed to feel that she was walking through hell.

She fled in utter terror, and at the end of the street she found the twilight sea again and the same stink of rotting shellfish as in the port of Riohacha, and her heart returned to its rightful place. She recognized the painted hotels along the deserted beach, the funereal taxis, the diamond of the first star in the immense sky. At the far end of the bay, solitary and enormous at the pier, its lights blazing on every deck, she recognized the ship on which she had sailed, and realized it no longer had anything to do with her life. She turned left at the corner but could not go on because of a crowd being held back by a squad of *carabinieri*. A row of ambulances waited with open doors outside her hotel building.

Standing on tiptoe and peering over the shoulders of the onlookers, Señora Prudencia Linero saw the English tourists again. They were being carried out on stretchers,

one by one, and all of them were motionless and dignified
and still seemed like one man repeated many times in the
more formal clothing they had put on for supper: flannel
trousers, diagonally striped ties, and dark jackets with the
Trinity College coat of arms embroidered on the breast
pocket. As they were brought out, the neighbors watching from their balconies, and the people held back on
the street, counted them in chorus as if they were in a
stadium. There were seventeen. They were put in the
ambulances two by two and driven away to the wail of
war sirens.

Dazed by so many stupefying events, Señora Prudencia
Linero rode up in the elevator packed with guests from
the other hotels who spoke in hermetic languages. They
got off at every floor except the third, which was open
and lit, but no one was at the counter or in the easy chairs
in the foyer where she had seen the pink knees of the
seventeen sleeping Englishmen. The owner on the fifth
floor commented on the disaster with uncontrolled ex-
citement.

"They're all dead," she told Señora Prudencia Linero
in Spanish. "They were poisoned by the oyster soup at
supper. Just imagine, oysters in August!"

She handed her the key to her room, and paid no further
attention to her as she said to the other guests in her own
dialect, "Since there's no dining room here, everyone
who goes to sleep wakes up alive!" With another knot of
tears in her throat, Señora Prudencia Linero bolted the
locks in her room. After that she pushed the little writing
table and the easy chair and her trunk against the door
to form an impassable barricade against the horror of a

country where so many things happened at the same time. Then she put on her widow's nightgown, lay down in the bed on her back, and said seventeen Rosaries for the eternal rest of the souls of the seventeen poisoned Englishmen.

APRIL 1980

Tramontana

I saw him only once at Boccacio, the popular Barcelona club, a few hours before his miserable death. It was two in the morning and he was being pursued by a gang of young Swedes attempting to take him away with them to finish the party in Cadaqués. There were eleven Swedes, and it was difficult to tell one from another because all of them, men and women, looked the same: beautiful, with narrow hips and long golden hair. He could not have been older than twenty. His head was covered with blue-black curls, and he had the smooth, sallow skin of Caribbeans whose mothers had trained them to walk in the shade, and Arab eyes that were enough to drive the Swedish girls mad, and perhaps a few of the boys as well. They had seated him on the bar, like a ventriloquist's dummy, and were serenading him with popular songs to the accompaniment of their clapping hands as they tried to persuade him to go with them.

In terror he attempted to explain his reasons. Someone intervened, shouting that they ought to leave him alone, and one of the Swedes, weak with laughter, confronted him.

"He's ours," he yelled. "We found him in the garbage can."

I had come in just a short while before with a group of friends, after attending David Oistrakh's final concert in the Palau de la Música, and my skin crawled at the skepticism of the Swedes. For the boy's reasons were sacred. He had lived in Cadaqués, where he had been hired to sing Antillean songs in a fashionable bar, until the previous summer, when the tramontana defeated him. He managed to escape on the second day, resolved never to return, with or without the tramontana, and certain that if he ever went back, death would be waiting for him. It was a Caribbean certainty that could not be understood by a band of Scandinavian rationalists aflame with summer and the hard Catalan wines of those days, which sowed wild ideas in the heart.

I understood him better than anyone. Cadaqués was one of the most beautiful towns along the Costa Brava, and one of the best preserved. This was due in part to the fact that its narrow access highway twisted at the edge of a bottomless abyss, and one needed a very steady soul to drive more than fifty kilometers an hour. The older houses were white and low, in the traditional style of Mediterranean fishing villages. The new ones had been built by famous architects who respected the original harmony. In summer, when the heat seemed to come from

African deserts on the other side of the street, Cadaqués turned into a hellish Babel, where for three months tourists from every corner of Europe vied with the natives, and with the foreigners who had been lucky enough to buy a house at a low price when that was still possible, for control of paradise. But in spring and fall, the seasons when Cadaqués seemed most attractive, no one could escape the terrifying thought of the tramontana, a harsh, tenacious land wind that carries in it the seeds of madness, according to the natives and certain writers who have learned their lesson.

Until the tramontana crossed our lives some fifteen years ago, I was one of the town's most faithful visitors. One Sunday at siesta time, with the unexplainable presentiment that something was about to happen, I sensed the wind before it arrived. My spirits plummeted, I felt sad for no reason, and I had the impression that my children, who were then both under ten years old, were following me around the house with hostile stares. Not long afterward the porter came in with a toolbox and some marine lines to secure the doors and windows, and he was not surprised at my dejection.

"It's the tramontana," he said. "It'll be here in less than an hour."

He was a very old man, a former seaman who still had the waterproof jacket of his trade, the cap and pipe, and a skin scorched by the salts of the world. In his free hours he would play bowls in the square with veterans of several lost wars, and drink aperitifs with tourists in the taverns along the beach, for with his artilleryman's Catalan he had the virtue of making himself understood in any language. He prided himself on knowing all the ports of the planet, but no inland city. "Not even Paris, France, as famous as it is," he would say. For he had no faith in any vehicle that did not sail.

In the last few years his aging had been drastic, and he had not gone back to the street. He spent most of his time in the porter's room, alone in spirit, as he had always lived. He cooked his own food in a can over an alcohol lamp, but that was all he needed to delight us with the delicacies of an illustrious cuisine. At dawn he would begin tending to the tenants, floor by floor, and he was one of the most accommodating men I have ever met, with the involuntary generosity and rough tenderness of the Catalonians. He spoke very little, but his style was direct and to the point. When he had nothing else to do, he spent hours filling out forms that predicted the outcome of soccer games, but he did not mail them in very often.

That day, as he secured the doors and windows in anticipation of the disaster, he spoke to us of the tramontana as if it were a hateful woman, but one without whom his life would lose its meaning. It surprised me that a sailor would pay such homage to a land wind.

"This is one of the old ones," he said.

He gave the impression that his year was not divided into days and months, but into the number of times the tramontana blew. "Last year, about three days after the second tramontana, I had an attack of colitis," he once told me. Perhaps this explained his belief that one aged several years after each tramontana. His obsession was so great that he filled us with a longing to get to know it, as if it were a fatal, seductive visitor.

We did not have long to wait. As soon as the porter left, we heard a whistling that little by little became sharper and more intense and dissolved into the thunder of an earthquake. Then the wind began. First in intermittent gusts that became more frequent until one of them remained, unmoving, without pause, without relief, with an intensity and cruelty that seemed supernatural. Contrary to Caribbean custom, our apartment faced the mountains, perhaps because of that peculiar preference of old-fashioned Catalonians who love the sea but do not care to look at it. And so the wind hit us head-on and threatened to blow away the ropes that moored the windows.

What intrigued me most was that the weather still had an unrepeatable beauty, with its golden sun and undaunted sky. So much so that I decided to take the children out to the street to have a look at the ocean. After all, they had been raised among Mexican earthquakes and Caribbean hurricanes, and one wind more or less did not seem anything to worry about. We tiptoed past the porter's room and saw him transfixed before a plate of beans and sausage, watching the wind through the window. He did not see us go out.

We managed to walk as long as we were on the lee side of the house, but when we reached the exposed corner we had to hold on to a lamppost in order not to be blown away by the force of the wind. And there we stayed, amazed at the motionless, clear ocean in the midst of the cataclysm, until the porter, with the help of some neighbors, came to our rescue. Then, at last, we were convinced that the only rational course of action was to remain in the house until God willed otherwise. And no one had the slightest idea when that would be.

At the end of two days we had the impression that the fearful wind was not a natural phenomenon but a personal affront aimed by someone at us, and us alone. The porter visited several times a day, concerned for our state of mind, and he brought fruits in season and candies for the children. At lunch on Tuesday he regaled us with rabbit and snails, the masterpiece of Catalonian cookery, which he had prepared in his kitchen tin. It was a party in the midst of horror.

Wednesday, when nothing happened except the wind, was the longest day of my life. But it must have been something like the dark before the dawn, because after midnight we all awoke at the same time, overwhelmed by an absolute stillness that could only be the silence of death. Not a leaf moved on the trees that faced the mountain. And so we went out to the street, before the light was on in the porter's room, and relished the predawn sky with all its stars shining, and the phosphorescent sea. Although it was not yet five o'clock, many tourists were celebrating their relief on the rocky beach, and sailboats were being rigged after three days of penance.

When we went out we paid no particular attention to the fact that the porter's room was dark. But when we returned to the house, the air was as phosphorescent as the ocean and his room was still dark. I thought it odd and knocked twice, and since there was no answer I pushed the door. I believe the children saw him before I did, and they screamed in horror. The old porter, the insignias of a distinguished mariner pinned to the lapel of his seaman's jacket, was hanging by his neck from the middle rafter and still swaying in the final gust of the tramontana.

In the middle of our vacation, feeling an anticipatory nostalgia and an irrevocable determination never to return, we left the village earlier than planned. The tourists were back in the streets, and there was music in the square, where the veterans were almost too discouraged to bowl one ball against the other. Through the dusty windows of the Marítim bar we caught a glimpse of some friends who had survived and were beginning life again in the brilliant tramontana spring. But now all of that belonged to the past.

That was why, in the sad hours before dawn at Boccacio, no one understood as well as I the terror of someone who refused to return to Cadaqués because he was sure he would die. But there was no way to dissuade the Swedes, who dragged the boy away with the European intention of curing him by force of his African superstitions. To the applause and boos of a divided clientele, they pushed him kicking into a van filled with drunks who started out at that late hour on the long drive to Cadaqués.

The next morning the telephone woke me. I had forgotten to close the curtains when I came home from the party, and had no idea of the time, but the bedroom was filled with brilliant summer light. The worried voice on the phone, which I did not recognize right away, pulled me out of sleep.

"Do you remember the boy they took to Cadaqués last night?"

I did not have to hear another word. Except that it was even more dramatic than I had imagined. The boy, terrified by his imminent return to Cadaqués, took advantage of a moment's carelessness on the part of the demented Swedes, and in an effort to escape an ineluctable death, threw himself from the speeding van into the abyss.

JANUARY 1982

Miss Forbes's
Summer of Happiness

WHEN WE CAME back to the house in the afternoon, we found an enormous sea serpent nailed by the
neck to the door frame. Black and phosphorescent, it
looked like a Gypsy curse with its still-flashing eyes and
its sawlike teeth in gaping jaws. I was about nine years
old at the time, and at the sight of that vision out of a
delirium I felt a terror so intense that I lost my voice. But
my brother, who was two years younger, dropped the
oxygen tanks, the masks, the fins, and fled, screaming in
panic. Miss Forbes heard him from the tortuous stone
steps that wound along the reefs from the dock to the
house, and she ran to us, panting and livid, yet she had
only to see the beast crucified on the door to understand
the cause of our horror. She always said that when two

children were together they were both guilty of what each did alone, and so she scolded the two of us for my brother's screams and continued to reprimand us for our lack of self-control. She spoke in German, not in the English stipulated in her tutor's contract, perhaps because she too was frightened and refused to admit it. But as soon as she caught her breath she returned to her stony English and her pedagogical obsession.

"It is a *Muraena helena*," she told us, "so called because it was an animal sacred to the ancient Greeks."

All at once Oreste, the local boy who taught us how to swim in deep waters, appeared behind the agave plants. He was wearing his diving mask on his forehead, a minuscule bathing suit, and a leather belt that held six knives of different shapes and sizes, for he could conceive of no other way to hunt underwater than by engaging in hand-to-hand combat with his prey. He was about twenty years old and spent more time at the bottom of the sea than on solid ground, and with motor oil always smeared over his body he even looked like a sea animal. When she saw him for the first time, Miss Forbes told my parents that it was impossible to imagine a more beautiful human being. But his beauty could not save him from her severity: He too had to endure a reprimand, in Italian, for having hung the moray eel on the door, with no other possible reason than his desire to frighten the children. Then Miss Forbes ordered him to take it down with the respect due a mythical creature, and told us to dress for supper.

We did so without delay, trying not to commit a single error, because after two weeks under the regime of Miss

Forbes we had learned that nothing was more difficult than living. As we showered in the dim light of the bathroom, I knew that my brother was still thinking about the moray. "It had people's eyes," he said. I agreed, but made him think otherwise and managed to change the subject until I finished washing. Yet when I stepped out of the shower he asked me to stay and keep him company.

"It's still daytime," I said.

I opened the curtains. It was the middle of August, and through the window you could see the burning lunar plain all the way to the other side of the island, and the sun that had stopped in the sky.

"That's not why," my brother said. "I'm just scared of being scared."

But when we came down to the table he seemed calm, and he had done everything with so much care that he earned special praise from Miss Forbes and two more points in the week's good-conduct report. I, on the other hand, lost two of the five points I had already earned, because at the last minute I permitted myself to hurry and came into the dining room out of breath. Every fifty points entitled us to a double portion of dessert, but neither of us had earned more than fifteen. It was a shame, really, because we never again tasted any desserts as delicious as those made by Miss Forbes.

Before beginning supper we would stand and pray behind our empty plates. Miss Forbes was not Catholic, but her contract stipulated that she would have us pray six times a day, and she had learned our prayers in order to fulfill those terms. Then the three of us would sit down, and we held our breath while she scrutinized our deportment down to the slightest detail, and only when everything seemed perfect would she ring the bell. Then the cook, Fulvia Flaminea, came in, carrying the eternal vermicelli soup of that abominable summer.

At first, when we were alone with our parents, meals were a fiesta. Fulvia Flaminea giggled all around the table as she served us, with a vocation for disorder that brought joy to our lives, and then sat down with us and ate a little bit from everyone's plate. But ever since Miss Forbes had taken charge of our destiny, she served in such dark silence that we could hear the bubbling of the soup as it boiled in the tureen. We ate with our spines against the back of our chairs, chewing ten times on one side and ten times on the other, never taking our eyes off the iron, languid, autumnal woman who recited etiquette lessons by heart. It was just like Sunday Mass, but without the consolation of people singing.

On the day we found the moray eel hanging from the door, Miss Forbes spoke to us of our patriotic obligations. After the soup, Fulvia Flaminea, almost floating on the air rarefied by our tutor's voice, served a broiled fillet of snowy flesh with an exquisite aroma. I have always preferred fish to any other food on land or in the sky, and that memory of our house in Guacamayal eased my heart. But my brother refused the dish without tasting it.

"I don't like it," he said.

Miss Forbes interrupted her lesson.

"You cannot know that," she told him. "You have not even tasted it."

She shot a warning glance at the cook, but it was too late.

"Moray is the finest fish in the world, *figlio mio*," Fulvia Flaminea told him. "Try it and see."

Miss Forbes remained calm. She told us, with her unmerciful methodology, that moray had been a delicacy of kings in antiquity and that warriors fought over its bile because it gave them supernatural courage. Then she repeated, as she had so often in so short a time, that good taste was not an innate faculty, nor was it taught at any particular age; rather, it was imposed from infancy. Therefore we had no valid reason not to eat. I had tasted the moray before I knew what it was, and remembered the contradiction forever after: It had a smooth, rather melancholy taste, yet the image of the serpent nailed to the door frame was more compelling than my appetite. My brother made a supreme effort with his first bite, but he could not bear it: He vomited.

"You will go to the bathroom," Miss Forbes told him without losing her calm, "you will wash yourself with care, and you will come back to eat."

I felt great anguish for him, because I knew how difficult he found it to cross the entire house in the early darkness and stay alone in the bathroom for the time he needed to wash. But he returned very soon in a clean shirt, pale and quivering with a hidden tremor, and he bore up very well under the rigorous inspection of his cleanliness. Then Miss Forbes sliced a piece of moray and ordered us to continue. I just managed a second bite. But my brother did not even pick up his knife and fork.

"I'm not going to eat it," he said.

His determination was so obvious that Miss Forbes withdrew.

"All right," she said, "but you will have no dessert."

My brother's relief filled me with his courage. I crossed my knife and fork on my plate, just as Miss Forbes had taught us to do when we were finished, and said:

"I won't have dessert either."

"And you will not watch television," she replied.

"And we will not watch television," I said.

Miss Forbes placed her napkin on the table, and the three of us stood to pray. Then she sent us to our bedroom, with the warning that we had to be asleep by the time she finished eating. All our good-conduct points were canceled, and only after we had earned twenty more would we again enjoy her cream cakes, her vanilla tarts, her exquisite plum pastries, the likes of which we would not taste again for the rest of our lives.

The break was bound to come sooner or later. For an entire year we had looked forward to a summer of freedom on the island of Pantelleria, at the far southern end of Sicily, and that is what it really had been for the first month, when our parents were with us. I still remember as if it were a dream the solar plain of volcanic rock, the eternal sea, the house painted with quicklime up to the brickwork; on windless nights you could see from its windows the luminous beams of lighthouses in Africa. Exploring the sleeping ocean floor around the island with our father, we had discovered a row of yellow torpedoes, half buried since the last war; we had brought up a Greek amphora almost a meter high, with petrified garlands and the dregs of an immemorial and poisonous wine in its depths; we had bathed in a steaming pool of waters so dense you almost could walk on them. But the most dazzling revelation for us had been Fulvia Flaminea. She looked like a cheerful bishop and was always accompanied by a troop of sleepy cats who got in her way when she walked. But she said she put up with them not out of love but to keep from being devoured by rats. At night, while our parents watched programs for adults on television, Fulvia Flaminea took us to her house, less than a hundred meters from ours, and taught us to distinguish the remote babbling, the songs, the outbursts of weeping on the winds from Tunis. Her husband was a man too young for her, who worked in the summer at the tourist hotels on the far end of the island and came home only to sleep. Oreste lived a little farther away with his parents, and always appeared at night with strings of fish and baskets of fresh-caught lobster, which he hung in the kitchen so that Fulvia Flaminea's husband could sell them the next day at the hotels. Then he would put his diving lantern back on his forehead and take us to catch the field rats as big as rabbits that lay in wait for kitchen scraps. Sometimes we came home after our parents had gone to bed, and it was hard for us to sleep with the racket the rats made as they fought over the garbage in the courtyards. But even that annoyance was a magical ingredient in our happy summer.

The decision to hire a German governess could have occurred only to my father, a writer from the Caribbean with more presumption than talent. Dazzled by the ashes of the glories of Europe, he always seemed too eager to excuse his origins, in his books as well as in real life, and he had succumbed to the fantasy that no vestige of his own past would remain in his children. My mother was still as unassuming as she had been when she was an itinerant teacher in Alta Guajira, and she never imagined her husband could have an idea that was less than providential. And therefore they could not have asked themselves in their hearts what our lives would be like with a sergeant from Dortmund intent on inculcating in us by force the most ancient, stale habits of European society, while they and forty other fashionable writers participated in a five-week cultural encounter on the islands of the Aegean Sea.

Miss Forbes arrived on the last Saturday in July on the regular boat from Palermo, and from the moment we first saw her we knew the party was over. She arrived in that southern heat wearing combat boots, a dress with overlapping lapels, and hair cut like a man's under her felt hat. She smelled of monkey urine. "That's how every European smells, above all in summer," our father told us. "It's the smell of civilization." But despite her military appearance, Miss Forbes was a poor creature who might have awakened a certain compassion in us if we had been older or if she had possessed any trace of tenderness. The world changed. Our six hours in the ocean, which from the beginning of the summer had been a continual exercise of our imagination, were turned into one identical hour repeated over and over again. When we were with our parents we had all the time we wanted to swim with Oreste and be astonished at the art and daring with which he confronted octopuses in their own environment murky with ink and blood, using no other weapons than his combat knives. He still arrived as always at eleven o'clock in his little outboard motorboat, but Miss Forbes did not allow him to stay with us a minute longer than required for our lesson in deep-sea diving. She forbade us to go to Fulvia Flaminea's house at night because she considered it excessive familiarity with servants, and we had to devote the hours we had once spent in the pleasurable hunting of rats to analytical readings of Shakespeare. Accustomed to stealing mangoes from courtyards and stoning dogs to death on the burning streets of Guacamayal, we could not imagine a crueler torture than that princely life.

But we soon realized that Miss Forbes was not as strict with herself as she was with us, and this was the first chink in her authority. In the beginning she stayed on the beach under the multicolored umbrella, dressed for war and reading ballads by Schiller, while Oreste taught us to dive, and then, for hours and hours, she gave us theoretical lectures on proper behavior in society, until it was time for lunch.

One day she asked Oreste to take her in his boat to the hotel tourist shops, and she came back with a one-piece bathing suit as black and iridescent as a sealskin, yet she never went in the water. She sunbathed on the beach while we swam, and wiped away the perspiration with a towel but did not take a shower, so that after three days she looked like a boiled lobster and the smell of her civilization had become unbreathable.

At night she gave vent to her emotions. From the very start of her reign we heard someone walking through the house, feeling his way in the darkness, and my brother was tormented by the idea that it was one of the wandering drowning victims that Fulvia Flaminea had told us so much about. We soon discovered, however, that it was Miss Forbes, who spent the night living her real life as a lonely woman, which she herself would have censured during the day. One morning at dawn we surprised her in the kitchen in her schoolgirl's nightdress, preparing her splendid desserts. Her entire body, including her face, was covered with flour, and she was drinking a glass of port with a mental abandon that would have scandalized the other Miss Forbes. By then we knew that after we were in bed she did not go to her bedroom but went down to swim in secret, or stayed in the living room until very late, watching movies forbidden to minors on television, with the sound turned off, eating entire cakes and even drinking from the bottle of special wine that my father saved with so much devotion for memorable occasions. In defiance of her own sermons on austerity and composure, she wolfed everything down, choking on it with a kind of uncontrolled passion. Later we heard her talking to herself in her room, we heard her reciting complete excerpts from *Die Jungfrau von Orleans* in melodious German, we heard her singing, we heard her sobbing in her bed until dawn, and then she would appear at breakfast, her eyes swollen with tears, more gloomy and authoritarian than ever. My brother and I were never again as unhappy as we were then, but I was prepared to endure her to the end, for I knew that in any case her word would prevail over ours. My brother, however, confronted her with all the force of his character, and the summer of happiness became hellish for us. The episode of the moray eel was the final straw. That same night, as we lay in our beds listening to the incessant coming and going of Miss Forbes in the sleeping house, my brother released all the hatred rotting in his soul.

"I'm going to kill her," he said.

I was surprised, not so much by his decision as by the fact that I had been thinking the same thing since supper. I tried, however, to dissuade him.

"They'll cut off your head," I told him.

"They don't have guillotines in Sicily," he said. "Besides, nobody will know who did it."

I thought about the amphora salvaged from the water, where the dregs of fatal wine still lay. My father had kept it because he wanted a more thorough analysis to determine the nature of the poison, which could not be the product of the simple passage of time. Using the wine on Miss Forbes would be so easy that nobody would think it was not an accident or suicide. And so at dawn, when we heard her collapse, exhausted by the rigors of her vigil, we poured wine from the amphora into my father's bottle of special wine. From what we had heard, that dose was enough to kill a horse.

We ate breakfast in the kitchen at nine o'clock sharp, Miss Forbes herself serving us the sweet rolls that Fulvia Flaminea left on the top of the stove very early in the morning. Two days after we had substituted the wine, while we were having breakfast, my brother let me know with a disillusioned glance that the poisoned bottle stood untouched on the sideboard. That was a Friday, and the bottle remained untouched over the weekend. Then on Tuesday night, Miss Forbes drank half the wine while she watched dissolute movies on television.

Yet on Wednesday she came to breakfast with her

customary punctuality. As usual, her face looked as if she had spent a bad night; as always, her eyes were uneasy behind the heavy glasses, and they became even more uneasy when she found a letter with German stamps in the basket of rolls. She read it while she drank her coffee, which she had told us so many times one must not do, and while she read, flashes of light radiating from the written words passed over her face. Then she removed the stamps from the envelope and put them in the basket with the remaining rolls so that Fulvia Flaminea's husband could have them for his collection. Despite her initial bad experience, she accompanied us that day in our exploration of the ocean depths, and we wandered through a sea of delicate water until the air in our tanks began to run out, and we went home without our lesson in good manners. Not only was Miss Forbes in a floral mood all day, but at supper she seemed even more animated. My brother, however, could not tolerate his disappointment. As soon as we received the order to begin, he pushed away the plate of vermicelli soup with a provocative gesture.

"This worm water gives me a pain in the ass," he said.

It was as if he had tossed a grenade on the table. Miss Forbes turned pale, her lips hardened until the smoke of the explosion began to clear away, and the lenses of her glasses blurred with tears. Then she took them off, dried them with her napkin, placed the napkin on the table with the bitterness of an inglorious defeat, and stood up.

"Do whatever you wish," she said. "I do not exist."

She was locked in her room from seven o'clock on. But before midnight, when she supposed we were asleep, we saw her pass by in her schoolgirl's nightdress, carrying half a chocolate cake and the bottle with more than four fingers of poisoned wine back to her bedroom. I felt a tremor of pity.

"Poor Miss Forbes," I said.

My brother did not breathe easy.

"Poor us if she doesn't die tonight," he said.

That night she talked to herself again for a long time, declaimed Schiller in a loud voice inspired by a frenetic madness, and ended with a final shout that filled the entire house. Then she sighed many times from the depths of her soul and succumbed with a sad, continuous whistle like a boat adrift. When we awoke, still exhausted by the tension of the night, the sun was cutting through the blinds but the house seemed submerged in a pond. Then we realized it was almost ten and we had not been awakened by Miss Forbes's morning routine. We did not hear the toilet flush at eight, or the faucet turn in the sink, or the noise of the blinds, or the metallic sound of her boots, or the three mortal blows on the door with the flat of her slave driver's hand. My brother put his ear to the wall, held his breath in order to detect the slightest sign of life from the next room, and at last breathed a sigh of liberation.

"That's it!" he said. "All you can hear is the ocean."

We prepared our breakfast a little before eleven, and then, before Fulvia Flaminea arrived with her troop of cats to clean the house, we went down to the beach with two air tanks each and another two as spares. Oreste was already on the dock, gutting a six-pound gilthead he had just caught. We told him we had waited for Miss Forbes until eleven, and since she was still sleeping we decided to come down to the ocean by ourselves. We told him too that she had suffered an attack of weeping at the table the night before, and perhaps she had not slept well and wanted to stay in bed. Just as we expected, Oreste was not very interested in our explanation, and he accompanied us on our pillaging of the ocean floor for a little more than an hour. Then he told us we should go up for lunch, and left in his boat to sell the gilthead at the tourist hotels. We waved good-bye from the stone steps, making him think we were about to climb up to the house, until he disappeared around the cliff. Then we put on our air tanks and continued to swim without anyone's permission.

The day was cloudy and there was a rumble of dark thunder on the horizon, but the sea was smooth and clear and its own light was enough. We swam on the surface to the line of the Pantelleria lighthouse, then turned a hundred meters to the right and dove at the spot where we calculated we had seen the torpedoes at the beginning of the summer. There they were: six of them, painted sun-yellow with their serial numbers intact, and lying on the volcanic bottom in an order too perfect to be accidental. We kept circling the lighthouse, looking for the submerged city that Fulvia Flaminea had told us about so often, and with so much awe, but we could not find it. After two hours, convinced there were no new mysteries to discover, we surfaced with our last gulp of oxygen.

A summer storm had broken while we were swimming, the sea was rough, and a flock of bloodthirsty birds flew with fierce screams over the trail of dying fish on the beach. Yet without Miss Forbes the afternoon light seemed brand-new and life was good. But when we finished struggling up the steps cut into the cliff, we saw a crowd of people at the house and two police cars by the door, and for the first time we were conscious of what we had done. My brother began to tremble and tried to turn back.

"I'm not going in," he said.

I, on the other hand, had the confused notion that if we just looked at the body we would be safe from all suspicion.

"Take it easy," I told him. "Take a deep breath, and think about just one thing: We don't know anything."

No one paid attention to us. We left our tanks, masks, and flippers at the gate and went to the side veranda, where two men sat on the floor next to a stretcher and smoked. Then we realized there was an ambulance at the back door, and several soldiers armed with rifles. In the living room women from the area were sitting on chairs that had been pushed against the wall and praying in dialect, while their men crowded into the courtyard talking about anything that did not have to do with death. I squeezed my brother's hard, icy hand even tighter, and we walked into the house through the back door. Our bedroom door was open, and the room was just as we had left it that morning. In Miss Forbes's room, which was next to ours, an armed *carabineriere* stood guarding the entrance, but the door was open. We walked toward it with heavy hearts, and before we had a chance to look in, Fulvia Flaminea came out of the kitchen like a bolt of lightning and shut the door with a scream of horror:

"For God's sake, *figlioli*, don't look at her!"

It was too late. Never, for the rest of our lives, would we forget what we saw in that fleeting instant. Two plain-clothesmen were measuring the distance from the bed to the wall with a tape, while another was taking pictures with a black-sleeve camera like the ones park photographers used. Miss Forbes was not on the unmade bed. She was stretched on her side, naked in a pool of dried blood that had stained the entire floor, and her body was riddled by stab wounds. There were twenty-seven fatal cuts, and by their number and brutality one could see that the attack had been made with the fury of a love that found no peace, and that Miss Forbes had received it with the same passion, without even screaming or crying, reciting Schiller in her beautiful soldier's voice, conscious of the fact that this was the inexorable price of her summer of happiness.

1976

Light Is Like Water

At CHRISTMAS the boys asked again for a rowboat.

"Okay," said their papa, "we'll buy it when we get back to Cartagena."

Totó, who was nine years old, and Joel, who was seven, were more determined than their parents believed.

"No," they said in chorus. "We need it here and now."

"To begin with," said their mother, "the only navigable water here is what comes out of the shower."

She and her husband were both right. Their house in Cartagena de Indias had a yard with a dock on the bay, and a shed that could hold two large yachts. Here in Madrid, on the other hand, they were crowded into a fifth-floor apartment at 47 Paseo de la Castellana. But in the end neither of them could refuse, because they had promised the children a rowboat complete with sextant and compass if they won their class prizes in elementary school, and they had. And so their papa bought everything and said nothing to his wife, who was more reluctant than he to pay gambling debts. It was a beautiful aluminum boat with a gold stripe at the waterline.

"The boat's in the garage," their papa announced at lunch. "The problem is, there's no way to bring it up in the elevator or by the stairs, and there's no more space available in the garage."

On the following Saturday afternoon, however, the boys invited their classmates to help bring the boat up the stairs, and they managed to carry it as far as the maid's room.

"Congratulations," said their papa. "Now what?"

"Now nothing," said the boys. "All we wanted was to have the boat in the room, and now it's there."

On Wednesday night, as they did every Wednesday, the parents went to the movies. The boys, lords and masters of the house, closed the doors and windows and broke the glowing bulb in one of the living room lamps. A jet of golden light as cool as water began to pour out of the broken bulb, and they let it run to a depth of almost three feet. Then they turned off the electricity, took out the rowboat, and navigated at will among the islands in the house.

This fabulous adventure was the result of a frivolous remark I made while taking part in a seminar on the poetry of household objects. Totó asked me why the light went on with just the touch of a switch, and I did not have the courage to think about it twice.

"Light is like water," I answered. "You turn the tap and out it comes."

And so they continued sailing every Wednesday night, learning how to use the sextant and the compass, until their parents came home from the movies and found them sleeping like angels on dry land. Months later, longing to go farther, they asked for complete skin-diving outfits: masks, fins, tanks, and compressed-air rifles.

"It's bad enough you've put a rowboat you can't use in the maid's room," said their father. "To make it even worse, now you want diving equipment too."

"What if we win the Gold Gardenia Prize for the first semester?" said Joel.

"No," said their mother in alarm. "That's enough."

Their father reproached her for being intransigent.

"These kids don't win so much as a nail when it comes to doing what they're supposed to," she said, "but to get what they want they're capable of taking it all, even the teacher's chair."

In the end the parents did not say yes or no. But in July, Totó and Joel each won a Gold Gardenia and the public recognition of the headmaster. That same afternoon, without having to ask again, they found the diving outfits in their original packing in their bedroom. And so the following Wednesday, while their parents were at the movies seeing *Last Tango in Paris*, they filled the apartment to a depth of two fathoms, dove like tame sharks under the furniture, including the beds, and salvaged from the bottom of the light things that had been lost in darkness for years.

At the end-of-the-year awards ceremony, the brothers were acclaimed as examples for the entire school and received certificates of excellence. This time they did not have to ask for anything, because their parents asked them what they wanted. They were so reasonable that all they wanted was a party at home as a treat for their classmates.

Their papa, when he was alone with his wife, was radiant.

"It's a proof of their maturity," he said.

"From your lips to God's ear," said their mother.

The following Wednesday, while their parents were watching *The Battle of Algiers*, people walking along the Paseo de la Castellana saw a cascade of light falling from an old building hidden among the trees. It spilled over the balconies, poured in torrents down the façade, and rushed along the great avenue in a golden flood that lit the city all the way to the Guadarrama.

In response to the emergency, firemen forced the door on the fifth floor and found the apartment brimming with light all the way to the ceiling. The sofa and easy chairs covered in leopard skin were floating at different levels in the living room, among the bottles from the bar and the grand piano with its Manila shawl that fluttered half submerged like a golden manta ray. Household objects, in the fullness of their poetry, flew with their own wings through the kitchen sky. The marching-band instruments that the children used for dancing drifted among the bright-colored fish freed from their mother's aquarium, which were the only creatures alive and happy in the vast illuminated marsh. Everyone's toothbrush floated in the bathroom, along with Papa's condoms and Mama's jars of creams and her spare bridge, and the television set from the master bedroom floated on its side, still tuned to the final episode of the midnight movie for adults only.

At the end of the hall, moving with the current and clutching the oars, with his mask on and only enough air to reach port, Totó sat in the stern of the boat, searching for the lighthouse, and Joel, floating in the prow, still looked for the north star with the sextant, and floating through the entire house were their thirty-seven classmates, eternalized in the moment of peeing into the pot of geraniums, singing the school song with the words changed to make fun of the headmaster, sneaking a glass of brandy from Papa's bottle. For they had turned on so many lights at the same time that the apartment had flooded, and two entire classes at the elementary school of Saint Julian the Hospitaler drowned on the fifth floor of 47 Paseo de la Castellana. In Madrid, Spain, a remote city of burning summers and icy winds, with no ocean or river, whose landbound indigenous population had never mastered the science of navigating on light.

DECEMBER 1978

The Trail of Your
Blood in the Snow

At nightfall, when they reached the frontier, Nena Daconte realized that her finger with the wedding band on it was still bleeding. The Civil Guardsman, a rough wool blanket covering his patent-leather tricorn hat, examined their passports in the light of a carbide lantern as he struggled to keep his footing in the fierce wind blowing out of the Pyrenees. Although the two diplomatic passports were in perfect order, the guard raised the lantern to make certain that the photographs resembled their faces. Nena Daconte was almost a child, with the eyes of a happy bird, and molasses skin still radiant with the bright Caribbean sun in the mournful January gloom, and she was wrapped up to her chin in a mink coat that could not have been bought with the year's wages of the entire frontier garrison. Her husband, Billy Sánchez de Ávila, who drove the car, was a year younger and almost as beautiful, and he wore a plaid jacket and a baseball hat. Unlike his wife, he was tall and athletic and had the iron jaw of a timid thug. But what best revealed the status of them both was the silver automobile whose interior exhaled a breath of living animal; nothing like it had ever been seen along that impoverished border. The rear seat overflowed with suitcases that were too new and many gift boxes that were still unopened. It also held the tenor saxophone that had been the overriding passion of Nena Daconte's life before she succumbed to the disquieting love of her tender beach hoodlum.

When the guard returned the stamped passports, Billy Sánchez asked him where they could find a pharmacy to treat his wife's finger, and the guard shouted into the wind that they should ask in Hendaye, on the French side. But the guards at Hendaye were inside a warm, well-lit glass sentry box, sitting at a table in their shirtsleeves and playing cards while they ate bread dipped in large glasses of wine, and all they had to see was the size and make of the car to wave them on into France. Billy Sánchez leaned on the horn several times, but the guards did not understand that he was calling them, and one of them opened the window and shouted with more fury than the wind:

"*Merde! Allez-vous-en!*"

Then Nena Daconte, wrapped in her coat up to her ears, got out of the car and asked the guard in perfect French where there was a pharmacy. As was his habit, the guard, his mouth full of bread, answered that it was no affair of his, least of all in a storm like this, and closed the window. But then he looked with more attention at the girl wrapped in the glimmer of natural mink and sucking her hurt finger, and he must have taken her for a magic vision on that fearful night, because his mood changed on the spot. He explained that the closest city was Biarritz, but in the middle of winter, and in that wind howling like wolves, they might not find a pharmacy open until Bayonne, a little farther on.

"Is it serious?" he asked.

"It's nothing," Nena Daconte said, smiling and showing him the finger with the diamond ring and the almost invisible scratch of the rose on the tip. "It was just a thorn."

Before they reached Bayonne, it began to snow again. It was no later than seven, but they found the streets deserted and the houses closed to the fury of the storm, and after turning many corners and not finding a pharmacy, they decided to drive on. The decision made Billy Sánchez happy. He had an insatiable passion for rare automobiles and a papa with too many feelings of guilt and more than enough resources to satisfy his whims, and he had never driven anything like the Bentley convertible that had been given to him as a wedding gift. His rapture at the wheel was so intense that the more he drove the less tired he felt. He wanted to reach Bordeaux that night. They had reserved the bridal suite at the Hôtel Splendid, and not all the contrary winds or snow in the sky could hold him back. Nena Daconte, on the other hand, was exhausted, in particular by the last stretch of highway from Madrid, which was the edge of a cliff fit for mountain goats and lashed by hailstorms. And so after Bayonne she wrapped a handkerchief around her ring finger, squeezing it tightly to stop the blood that was still flowing, and fell into a deep sleep. Billy Sánchez did not notice until close to midnight, when the snow had ended and the wind in the pines stopped all at once and the sky over the pastureland filled with glacial stars. He had passed the sleeping lights of Bordeaux but stopped only to fill the tank at a station along the highway, for he still had the energy to drive to Paris without a break. He was so delighted with his big, £25,000 toy that he did not even ask himself if the radiant creature asleep at his side—the bandage on her ring finger soaked with blood and her adolescent dream pierced for the first time by lightning flashes of uncertainty—felt the same way too.

They had been married three days before and ten thousand kilometers away, in Cartagena de Indias, to the astonishment of his parents and the disillusionment of hers, and with the personal blessing of the archbishop. No one except the two of them understood the real basis or knew the origins of that unforeseeable love. It had begun three months before the wedding, on a Sunday by the sea, when Billy Sánchez's gang had stormed the women's dressing rooms at the Marbella beaches. Nena had just turned eighteen; she had come home from the Châtellenie school in Saint-Blaise, Switzerland, speaking four languages without an accent, and with a masterful knowledge of the tenor saxophone, and this was her first Sunday at the beach since her return. She had stripped to the skin and was about to put on her bathing suit when the panicked stampede and pirate yells broke out in the nearby cabanas, but she did not understand what was going on until the latch on her door splintered and she saw the most beautiful bandit imaginable standing in front of her. He wore nothing but a pair of fake leopard-skin string briefs, and he had the peaceful, elastic body and golden color of those who live by the ocean. Around his right wrist he wore the metal bracelet of a Roman gladiator, and around his right fist he had coiled an iron chain that he used as a lethal weapon, and around his neck hung a medal with no saint, which throbbed in silence to the pounding of his heart. They had attended the same elementary school and broken many piñatas at the same birthday parties, for they both came from the provincial families that had ruled the city's destiny at will since colonial days, but they had not seen each other for so many years that at first they did not recognize one another. Nena Daconte remained standing, motionless, doing nothing to hide her intense nakedness. Then Billy Sánchez carried out his puerile ritual: He lowered his leopard-skin briefs and showed her his respectable erected manhood. She looked straight at it, with no sign of surprise.

"I've seen them bigger and harder," she said, controlling her terror. "So think again about what you're doing, because with me you'll have to perform better than a black man."

In reality not only was Nena Daconte a virgin, but until that moment she had never seen a naked man, yet her challenge was effective. All that Billy Sánchez could think to do was to smash the fist rolled in chain against the wall and break his hand. She drove him to the hospital in her car and helped him endure his convalescence, and in the end they learned together how to make love the correct way. They spent the difficult June afternoons on the interior terrace of the house where six generations of Nena Daconte's illustrious ancestors had died; she played popular songs on the saxophone, and he, with his hand in a cast, contemplated her from the hammock in unrelieved stupefaction. The house had countless floor-to-ceiling windows that faced the fetid stillwater of the bay, and it was one of the largest and oldest in the district of La Manga, and beyond any doubt the ugliest. But the terrace with the checkered tiles where Nena Daconte played the saxophone was an oasis in the four-o'clock heat, and it opened onto a courtyard with generous shade and mango trees and banana plants, under which there was a grave and a nameless tombstone older than the house and the family's memory. Even those who knew nothing about music thought the saxophone was an anachronism in so noble a house. "It sounds like a ship," Nena Daconte's grandmother had said when she heard it for the first time. Nena Daconte's mother had tried in vain to have her play it another way and not, for the sake of comfort, with her skirt up around her thighs and her knees apart, and with a sensuality that did not seem essential to the music. "I don't care what instrument you play," she would say, "as long as you play it with your legs together."

But those ship's farewell songs and that feasting on love were what allowed Nena Daconte to break the bitter shell around Billy Sánchez. Beneath his sad reputation as an ignorant brute, which he had upheld with great success because of the confluence of two illustrious family names, she discovered a frightened, tender orphan. While the bones in his hand were knitting, she and Billy Sánchez learned to know each other so well that even he was amazed at the fluidity with which love occurred when she took him to her virgin's bed one rainy afternoon when they were alone in the house. Every day at the same time, for almost two weeks, they caroused, passionate and naked, beneath the astonished gaze of the portraits of civil warriors and insatiable grandmothers who had preceded them in the paradise of that historic bed. Even in the pauses between love they remained naked and kept the windows open, breathing the air of ships' garbage wafting in from the bay, its smell of shit, and listening in the silence of the saxophone to the daily sounds from the courtyard, the single note of the frog beneath the banana plants, the drop of water falling on nobody's grave, the natural movements of life that they had not had the opportunity to learn before.

When her parents returned home, Nena Daconte and Billy Sánchez had progressed so far in love that the world was not big enough for anything else, and they made love anytime, anyplace, trying to reinvent it each time they did. At first they struggled in the sports cars with which Billy Sánchez's papa tried to quiet his own feelings of guilt. Then, when the cars became too easy for them, they would go at night into the deserted cabanas of Marbella where destiny had first brought them together, and during the November carnival they even went in costume to the rooms for hire in the old slave district of Getsemaní, under the protection of the matrons who until a few months before had been obliged to endure Billy Sánchez and his chain-wielding gang. Nena Daconte gave herself over to furtive love with the same frenetic devotion that she had once wasted on the saxophone, until her tamed bandit at last understood what she had meant when she said he would have to perform like a black man. Billy Sánchez always returned her love, with skill and the same enthusiasm. When they were married, they fulfilled their vow to love each other over the Atlantic, while the stewardesses slept and they were crammed into the airplane lavatory, overcome more by laughter than by pleasure. Only they knew then, twenty-four hours after the wedding, that Nena Daconte had been pregnant for two months.

And so when they reached Madrid they were far from being two sated lovers, but they had enough discretion to behave like pure newlyweds. Their parents had arranged everything. Before they left the plane, a protocol officer came to the first-class cabin to give Nena Daconte the white mink coat with gleaming black trim that was her wedding present from her parents. He gave Billy Sánchez the kind of shearling jacket that was all the rage that winter, and the unmarked keys to a surprise car waiting for him at the airport.

Their country's diplomatic mission welcomed them in the official reception room. Not only were the ambassador and his wife old friends of both families, but he was the doctor who had delivered Nena Daconte, and he was waiting for her with a bouquet of roses so radiant and fresh that even the dewdrops seemed artificial. She greeted them both with false kisses, uncomfortable with her somewhat premature status as bride, and then accepted the roses. As she took them she pricked her finger on a thorn, but she handled the mishap with a charming ruse.

"I did it on purpose," she said, "so you'd notice my ring."

In fact, the entire diplomatic mission marveled at the splendor of the ring, which must have cost a fortune, not so much because of the quality of the diamonds as for its well-preserved antiquity. But no one noticed that her finger had begun to bleed. They all turned their attention to the new car. The ambassador's amusing idea had been to bring it to the airport and have it wrapped in cellophane and tied with an enormous gold ribbon. Billy Sánchez did not even notice his ingenuity. He was so eager to see the car that he tore away the wrapping all at once and stood there breathless. It was that year's Bentley convertible, with genuine leather upholstery. The sky looked like a blanket of ashes, a cutting, icy wind blew out of the Guadarrama, and it was not a good time to be outside, but Billy Sánchez still had no notion of the cold. He kept the diplomatic mission in the outdoor parking lot, unaware that they were freezing for the sake of courtesy, until he finished looking over the smallest details of the car. Then the ambassador sat beside him to direct him to the official residence, where a luncheon had been prepared. En route he pointed out the most famous sights in the city, but Billy Sánchez seemed attentive only to the magic of the car.

It was the first time he had traveled outside his country. He had gone through all the private and public schools, repeating courses over and over again, until he was left adrift in a limbo of indifference. The initial sight of a city other than his own, the blocks of ashen houses with their lights on in the middle of the day, the bare trees, the distant ocean, everything increased a feeling of desolation that he struggled to keep in a corner of his heart. But soon he fell, without being aware of it, into the first trap of forgetting. A sudden, silent storm, the earliest of the season, had broken overhead, and when they left the ambassador's residence after lunch to begin their drive to France, they found the city covered with radiant snow. Then Billy Sánchez forgot the car, and with everyone watching he shouted with joy, threw fistfuls of snow over his head, and wearing his new coat, rolled on the ground in the middle of the street.

Nena Daconte did not realize that her finger was bleeding until they left Madrid on an afternoon that had turned transparent after the storm. It surprised her, because when she had accompanied the ambassador's wife, who liked to sing Italian arias after official luncheons, on the saxophone, her ring finger had hardly bothered her. Later, while she was telling her husband the shortest routes to the border, she sucked her finger in an unconscious way each time it bled, and only when they reached the Pyrenees did she think of looking for a pharmacy. Then she succumbed to the overdue dreams of the past few days, and when she awoke with a start to the nightmarish impression that the car was going through water, it was a long while before she remembered the handkerchief wrapped around her finger. She saw on the illuminated clock on the dashboard that it was after three, made her mental calculations, and only then realized that they had passed Bordeaux, as well as Angoulême and Poitiers, and were driving along the flooded dike of the Loire. Moonlight filtered through the mist, and the silhouettes of castles through the pines seemed to come from fairy tales. Nena Daconte, who knew the region by heart, estimated that they were about three hours from Paris, and Billy Sánchez, undaunted, was still at the wheel.

"You're a wild man," she said. "You've been driving for more than eleven hours and you haven't eaten a thing."

The intoxication of the new car kept him going. He had not slept very much on the plane, but he felt wide awake and energetic enough to be in Paris by dawn.

"I'm still full from the embassy lunch," he said. And he added, with no apparent logic, "After all, in Cartagena they're just leaving the movies. It must be about ten o'clock."

Even so, Nena Daconte was afraid he would fall asleep at the wheel. She opened one of the many presents they had received in Madrid and tried to put a piece of candied orange in his mouth. But he turned away.

"Real men don't eat sweets," he said.

A little before Orléans the fog cleared, and a very large moon lit the snow-covered fields, but traffic became more difficult because enormous produce trucks and wine tankers merged onto the highway, all heading for Paris. Nena Daconte would have liked to help her husband with the driving, but she did not dare even to suggest it: He had informed her the first time they went out together that nothing is more humiliating for a man than to be driven by his wife. She felt clearheaded after almost five hours of sound sleep, and she was happy too that they had not stopped at a hotel in the French provinces, which she had known since she was a little girl making countless trips

there with her parents. "There's no more beautiful countryside in the world," she said, "but you can die of thirst
and not find anyone who'll give you a free glass of water."
She was so convinced of this that at the last minute she
had put a cake of soap and a roll of toilet paper in her
overnight bag, because in French hotels there was never
any soap, and the paper in the bathrooms was last week's
newspapers cut into little squares and hung from a nail.
The only thing she regretted at that moment was having
wasted an entire night without making love. Her husband's reply was immediate.

"I was just thinking it must be fantastic to fuck in the
snow," he said. "Right here, if you want."

Nena Daconte gave it serious thought. The moonlit
snow at the edge of the highway looked fluffy and warm,
but as they approached the suburbs of Paris the traffic
grew heavier, and there were clusters of lit factories and
numerous workers on bicycles. If it had not been winter,
it would have been broad daylight by now.

"We'd better wait until Paris," said Nena Daconte.
"All nice and warm in a bed with clean sheets, like married people."

"It's the first time you've turned me down," he said.

"Of course," she replied. "It's the first time we've been
married."

A little before dawn they washed their faces and urinated at a roadside restaurant and had coffee with warm
croissants at the counter, where truck drivers drank red
wine with breakfast. In the bathroom Nena Daconte
saw that she had bloodstains on her blouse and skirt, but
she did not try to wash them out. She tossed her blood-

soaked handkerchief into the trash, moved her wedding ring to her left hand, and washed the wounded finger with soap and water. The scratch was almost invisible. Yet as soon as they were back in the car it began to bleed again, and Nena Daconte hung her arm out the window, certain that the icy air from the fields had cauterizing properties. This tactic proved useless too, but she was still unconcerned. "If anyone wants to find us it'll be very easy," she said with her natural charm. "All they have to do is follow the trail of my blood in the snow." Then she thought more about what she had said, and her face bloomed in the first light of dawn.

"Imagine," she said. "A trail of blood in the snow all the way from Madrid to Paris. Wouldn't that make a good song?"

She did not have time to think again. In the suburbs of Paris her finger bled in an uncontrollable flood, and she felt as if her soul were escaping through the scratch. She had tried to stop the flow with the toilet paper she carried in her bag, but it took longer to wrap her finger than to throw the strips of bloody paper out the window. The clothes she was wearing, her coat, the car seats were all becoming soaked, in a gradual but irreparable process. Billy Sánchez became really frightened and insisted on looking for a pharmacy, but by then she knew this was no matter for pharmacists.

"We're almost at the Porte d'Orléans," she said. "Go straight ahead, along Avenue Général Leclerc, the big one with all the trees, and then I'll tell you what to do."

This was the most difficult part of the trip. The Avenue du Général Leclerc was jammed in both directions, an infernal knot of small cars and motorcycles and the enormous trucks that were trying to reach the central markets. The useless clamor of the horns made Billy Sánchez so agitated that he shouted insults in chain-wielding language at several drivers and even tried to get out of the car to hit one of them, but Nena Daconte managed to convince him that although the French were the rudest people in the world, they never had fistfights. It was one more proof of her good judgment, because at that moment Nena Daconte was struggling not to lose consciousness.

It took them more than an hour just to get around the Léon de Belfort traffic circle. Cafés and stores were lit as if it were midnight, for it was a typical Tuesday in an overcast, filthy Parisian January, with a persistent rain that never solidified into snow. But there was less traffic on the Avenue Denfert-Rochereau, and after a few blocks Nena Daconte told her husband to turn right, and he parked outside the emergency entrance of a huge, gloomy hospital.

She had to be helped out of the car, yet she did not lose her calm or her lucidity. As she lay on the gurney waiting for the doctor on duty, she answered the nurse's routine questions regarding her identity and medical history. Billy Sánchez carried her bag and gripped her left hand, where she was wearing her wedding ring; it felt languid and cold, and her lips had lost their color. He stayed at her side, holding her hand, until the doctor arrived and made a brief examination of her wounded finger. He was a very young man with a shaved head and skin the color of old copper. Nena Daconte paid no attention to him, but turned a livid smile on her husband.

"Don't be afraid," she said, with her invincible humor. "The only thing that can happen is that this cannibal will cut off my hand and eat it."

The doctor completed his examination, then surprised them by speaking very correct Spanish with a strange Asian accent.

"No, children," he said. "This cannibal would rather die of hunger than cut off so beautiful a hand."

They were embarrassed, but the doctor calmed them with a good-natured gesture. Then he ordered the cot wheeled away, and Billy Sánchez tried to follow, clutching his wife's hand. The doctor took his arm and stopped him.

"Not you," he said. "She's going to intensive care."

Nena Daconte smiled again at her husband, and continued waving good-bye until she disappeared from sight at the end of the corridor. The doctor stayed behind, studying the information that the nurse had written on a clipboard. Billy Sánchez called to him.

"Doctor," he said. "She's pregnant."

"How far along?"

"Two months."

The doctor did not give this fact as much importance as Billy Sánchez had expected. "You were right to tell me," he said, and walked after the cot. Billy Sánchez was left standing in the mournful room that smelled of sick people's sweat, was left not knowing what to do as he looked down the empty corridor where they had taken Nena Daconte, and then he sat down on the wooden bench where other people were waiting. He did not know how long he sat there, but when he decided to leave the

176

hospital it was night again and still raining, and oppressed by the weight of the world, he still did not know what to do.

Nena Daconte was admitted at nine-thirty on Tuesday, January 7, as I learned years later from the hospital records. That first night, Billy Sánchez slept in the car, which was parked outside the emergency entrance, and very early the next day he ate six boiled eggs and drank two cups of café au lait in the closest cafeteria he could find, for he had not had a full meal since Madrid. Then he went back to the emergency room to see Nena Daconte, but they managed to make him understand that he had to use the main entrance. There, at last, an Asturian maintenance man helped him communicate with the receptionist, who in fact confirmed that Nena Daconte had been admitted to the hospital, but that visitors were allowed only on Tuesdays, from nine to four. That is, not for another six days. He tried to see the doctor who spoke Spanish, whom he described as a black man with a shaved head, but nobody could tell him anything on the basis of two such simple details.

Reassured by the news that Nena Daconte was in the registry, he returned to the car. A traffic officer made him park two blocks away, in a very narrow street, on the even-numbered side. Across the street was a renovated building with a sign: "Hôtel Nicole." It had only one star, and the reception area was very small, with just a sofa and an old upright piano, but the owner, whose voice was high and fluty, could understand clients in any language as long as they had money. Billy Sánchez with his eleven suitcases and nine gift boxes took the only free room, a triangular garret on the ninth floor, which he came to after a breathless climb up a circular staircase that smelled of boiled cauliflower. The walls were covered with a sad paper, and there was no room at the one window for anything but the dim light from an interior courtyard. There was a double bed, a large armoire, a straight-backed chair, a portable bidet, and a washstand with a bowl and pitcher, so that the only way to be in the room was to lie on the bed. Worse than old, everything was forlorn, but very clean, and with a salutary odor of recent medicine.

If he had spent the rest of his life in the attempt, Billy Sánchez could not have deciphered the enigmas of that world founded on a talent for miserliness. He never solved the mystery of the stairway light that went out before he reached his floor, and he never discovered how to turn it on again. He needed half a morning to learn that on the landing of each floor there was a little room with a toilet that one flushed by pulling a chain, and he already had decided to use it in the dark, when he discovered by accident that the light went on when the lock was bolted on the inside, so that no one would forget to turn it off again. The shower, which was at the end of the hall, and which he insisted on using twice a day as he did in his own country, one paid for separately, and in cash, and the hot water, controlled from the office, ran out in three minutes. Yet Billy Sánchez was thinking with sufficient clarity to realize that this way of doing things, so different from his own, was in any case better than being outdoors in January, and he felt so confused and alone that he could not understand how he ever had lived without the help and protection of Nena Daconte.

When he went up to his room on Wednesday morning, he threw himself facedown on the bed with his coat on, thinking about the miraculous creature who was still bleeding two blocks away, and he soon fell into so natural a sleep that when he awoke his watch said five o'clock, but he could not tell whether it was afternoon or morning, or what day of the week it was, or what city, with windows lashed by wind and rain. He waited, awake in the bed, always thinking about Nena Daconte, until he confirmed that in fact day was breaking. Then he went to have breakfast in the same cafeteria as the day before, and there he learned it was Thursday. The lights in the hospital were on and it had stopped raining, and so he leaned against the trunk of a chestnut tree outside the main entrance, where doctors and nurses in white coats walked in and out, hoping he would see the Asian physician who had admitted Nena Daconte. He did not see him then, or that afternoon after lunch, when he had to end his vigil because he was freezing. At seven he had another café au lait and two hard-boiled eggs that he chose from the display counter himself after two days of eating the same thing in the same place. When he went back to the hotel to sleep, he found his car alone on one side of the street, with a parking ticket on the windshield, while all the others were parked on the opposite side. It was a difficult task for the porter at the Hôtel Nicole to explain to him that on odd-numbered days one could park on the odd-numbered side of the street, and on even-

numbered days on the other side. Such rationalist strata-
gems proved incomprehensible to a purebred Sánchez
de Ávila, who almost two years before had driven the
mayor's official car into a neighborhood movie theater
and wreaked absolute havoc while the intrepid police
stood by. He understood even less when the porter ad-
vised him to pay the fine but not to move his car at that
hour, because he only would have to move it again at
midnight. As he tossed and turned on the bed and could
not sleep, he thought for the first time not only about
Nena Daconte, but about his own grievous nights in the
gay bars at the public market in Cartagena of the Caribbean. He remembered the taste of fried fish and coconut
rice in the restaurants along the dock, where the schooners
from Aruba moored. He remembered his house, the walls
covered with heartsease, where it would be just seven
o'clock the night before, and he saw his papa in silk
pajamas reading the newspaper in the coolness of the
terrace.

He remembered his mother—no one ever seemed to
know where she was, regardless of the hour—his desir-
able, talkative mother, who wore a Sunday dress and a
rose behind her ear when night fell, stifling with heat in
the encumbrance of splendid fabric. One afternoon when
he was seven years old, he had gone into her room without knocking and found her naked in bed with one of her
casual lovers. That mishap, which they had never men-
tioned, established a complicitous relationship between
them that proved more useful than love. But he was not
conscious of that, or of so many other terrible things in
his only child's loneliness, until the night he found him-

self tossing in the bed of a sad Parisian garret, with no one to tell his sorrows to, and in a fierce rage with himself because he could not bear his desire to cry.

It was a beneficial insomnia. He got out of bed on Friday wounded by the evil night he had spent, but determined to give definition to his life. He decided at last to break the lock on his suitcase and change his clothes, since all the keys were in Nena Daconte's bag, along with most of their money and the address book where, perhaps, he might have found the number of someone they knew in Paris. At his usual cafeteria he realized that he had learned to say hello in French, and to ask for ham sandwiches and café au lait. He knew it never would be possible to order butter or any kind of eggs because he never would learn to pronounce the words, but butter was always served with the bread, and the hard-boiled eggs were displayed on the counter, where he could take them without having to ask for them. Moreover, by the third day, the waiters recognized him and helped when he tried to make himself understood. And so at lunch on Friday, as he was trying to set his head to rights, he ordered a veal fillet with fried potatoes and a bottle of wine. He felt so good then that he ordered another bottle, drank almost half of it, and crossed the street with the firm resolve to force his way into the hospital. He did not know where to find Nena Daconte, but the providential image of the Asian doctor was fixed in his mind, and he was sure he would find him. He did not go in through the main door but used the emergency entrance, which had seemed less well guarded to him, but he could not get past the corridor where Nena Daconte had waved good-bye.

A guard with a blood-spattered smock asked him something as he walked by, and he paid no attention. The man followed him, repeating the same question over and over in French, and at last grabbed him by the arm with so much force that he stopped him short. Billy Sánchez tried to shake him off with a chain-wielder's trick, and then the guard shit on his mother in French, twisted his arm at the shoulder into a hammerlock, and without forgetting to shit a thousand times on his whore of a mother almost carried him to the door, raging with pain, and tossed him out into the middle of the street like a sack of potatoes.

That afternoon, aching with the punishment he had received, Billy Sánchez began to be an adult. He decided, as Nena Daconte would have done, to turn to his ambassador. The hotel porter, who despite his unsociable appearance was very helpful and very patient with languages, found the number and address of the embassy in the telephone book and wrote them down on a card. A very amiable woman answered the phone, and in no time Billy Sánchez recognized the diction of the Andes in her slow, colorless voice. He started by identifying himself, using his full name, certain the two great families would impress the woman, but the voice on the telephone did not change. He heard her recite her lesson by heart: His Excellency the Ambassador was not in his office at the moment and was not expected until the next day, but in any event he could be seen only by appointment, and then only under extraordinary circumstances. Billy Sánchez knew he would not find Nena Daconte by this route either, and he thanked the woman for the information with as much amiability as she had used in giving it. Then he took a taxi and went to the embassy.

It was at 22 Rue des Champs-Élysées, in one of the quietest districts in Paris, but the only thing that impressed Billy Sánchez, as he himself told me in Cartagena de Indias many years later, was that for the first time since his arrival the sunshine was as bright as in the Caribbean, and the Eiffel Tower loomed over the city against a radiant sky. The functionary who received him in the name of the ambassador looked as if he had just recovered from a fatal disease, not only because of his black suit, oppressive collar, and mourning tie, but also because of his judicious gestures and hushed voice. He understood Billy Sánchez's concern but reminded him, without losing any of his discretion, that they were in a civilized country whose strict norms were founded on the most ancient and learned criteria, in contrast to the barbaric Americas, where all one had to do to go into a hospital was bribe the porter. "No, dear boy," he said. His only recourse was to submit to the rule of reason and wait until Tuesday.

"After all, there are only four days left," he concluded. "In the meantime, go to the Louvre. It is worth seeing."

When he went out, Billy Sánchez found himself on the Place de la Concorde without knowing what to do. He saw the Eiffel Tower above the rooftops, and it seemed so close that he tried to walk there along the quays. But he soon realized it was farther than it appeared and kept changing position as he looked for it. And so he began to think about Nena Daconte as he sat on a bench along the Seine. He watched the tugs pass under the bridges, and to him they did not look like boats but itinerant houses, with red roofs and flower pots on the windowsills and clotheslines stretched across the deck. For a long while he watched a motionless fisherman, with a motionless rod and a motionless line in the current, and he tired of waiting for something to move, until it started growing dark and he decided to take a taxi back to the hotel. That was when he realized he did not know its name or address and had no idea where in Paris the hospital was located.

Stupefied by panic, he went into the first café he came to, asked for a cognac, and tried to put his thoughts in order. While he was thinking he saw himself repeated over and over and from many different angles in the numerous mirrors on the walls, saw that he was frightened and alone, and for the first time since the day of his birth he thought about the reality of death. But with the second glass of cognac he felt better, and had the providential idea of returning to the embassy. He looked in his pocket for the card with its address, and discovered that the name and street number of the hotel were printed on the other side. He was so shaken by the experience that he did not leave his room again for the entire weekend except to eat and move the car from one side of the street to the other. For three days the same filthy rain that had been falling the morning they had arrived continued to fall. Billy Sánchez, who had never read an entire book, wished he had one to fend off his boredom as he lay on the bed, but the only books he found in his wife's suitcases were in languages other than Spanish. And so he kept waiting for Tuesday, contemplating the peacocks repeated across the wallpaper and always thinking about Nena Daconte. On Monday he straightened the room, wondering what she would say if she found it in that state, and only then did he discover that the mink coat was stained with dried blood. He spent the afternoon washing it with the perfumed soap he found in her overnight bag, until he succeeded in restoring it to what it had been when it was carried onto the airplane in Madrid.

Tuesday dawned overcast and icy, but without the rain. Billy Sánchez was up at six and waited at the hospital entrance with a throng of relatives bringing gifts and bouquets of flowers to the patients. He went in with the crowd, carrying the mink coat over his arm, asking no questions and with no idea where Nena Daconte could be, but sustained by the certainty that he would meet the Asian doctor. He walked through a very large interior courtyard, with flowers and wild birds, and on each side were the wards: women to the right and men to the left. Following the other visitors, he entered the women's ward. He saw a long line of female patients in hospital gowns sitting on their beds, illuminated by the great light of the windows, and he even thought it was all much more cheerful than one could imagine from the outside. He reached the end of the corridor and then walked back, until he was certain that none of the patients was Nena Daconte. Then he walked around the exterior gallery again, peering through the windows at the men's ward, until he thought he recognized the doctor he was looking for.

And in fact he had. The doctor was examining a patient with some other doctors and several nurses. Billy Sánchez went into the ward, moved one of the nurses away from the group, and stood facing the Asian doctor, who was bent over the patient. He spoke to him. The doctor raised his sorrowful eyes, thought a moment, then recognized him.

"But where the hell have you been?" he asked.

Billy Sánchez was perplexed.

"In the hotel," he said. "Right here, around the corner."

Then he found out. Nena Daconte had bled to death at ten minutes past seven on the evening of Thursday, January 9, after sixty hours of failed efforts by the most qualified specialists in France. She had been lucid and serene to the end, instructing them to look for her husband at the Plaza-Athénée, where she and Billy Sánchez had a reservation, and giving them the necessary information for reaching her parents. The embassy had been informed by an urgent cable from the Foreign Office on Friday, when Nena Daconte's parents were already flying to Paris. The ambassador himself took care of the formalities for the embalming and the funeral, and stayed in touch with the police prefecture in Paris during the efforts to locate Billy Sánchez. An emergency bulletin with his description was broadcast from Friday night to Sunday afternoon over radio and television, and during those forty hours he was the most wanted man in France. His photograph, found in Nena Daconte's handbag, was displayed everywhere. Three Bentley convertibles of the same model had been located, but none of them was his.

Nena Daconte's parents had arrived at noon on Saturday and sat with the body in the hospital chapel, hoping until the last minute that Billy Sánchez would be found. His parents also had been informed and were ready to fly to Paris, but in the end they did not because of some confusion in the telegrams. The funeral took place on Sunday at two in the afternoon, only two hundred meters from the sordid hotel room where Billy Sánchez lay in agonies of loneliness for the love of Nena Daconte. The functionary who had received him at the embassy told me years later that he himself received the telegram from the Foreign Office an hour after Billy Sánchez left his office, and went to look for him in the discreet bars along the Rue du Faubourg-Saint-Honoré. He confessed to me that he had not paid much attention to Billy Sánchez when he saw him, because he never imagined that the boy from the coast, dazzled by the novelty of Paris and wearing such an unbecoming shearling coat, could have so illustrious an origin in his favor.

On the same night when he endured his desire to cry with rage, Nena Daconte's parents called off the search and took away the embalmed body in the metal coffin, and those who saw it repeated over and over again for many years that they never had seen a more beautiful woman, dead or alive. And therefore when Billy Sánchez at last entered the hospital on Tuesday morning, the burial had already taken place in the mournful cemetery of La Manga, a few meters from the house where they had deciphered the first keys to their happiness. The Asian doctor who told Billy Sánchez about the tragedy wanted to give him some tranquilizers in the hospital waiting room, but he refused. Billy Sánchez left without saying good-bye, without anything to say thank you for, thinking that the only thing he needed with great urgency was to find somebody and beat his brains out with a chain in revenge for his own misfortune. When he walked out of the hospital, he did not even realize that snow with no trace of blood was falling from the sky, in tender, bright flakes that looked like the downy feathers of doves, or that there was a festive air on the streets of Paris, because it was the first big snowfall in ten years.

1976

A Note About the Author

Gabriel García Márquez was born in Aracataca, Colombia, in 1928. He attended the University of Bogotá and later worked as a reporter for the Colombian newspaper *El Espectador* and as a foreign correspondent in Rome, Paris, Barcelona, Caracas, and New York. The author of several novels and collections of stories—including *No One Writes to the Colonel and Other Stories*, *The Autumn of the Patriarch*, *Innocent Eréndira and Other Stories*, *In Evil Hour*, *Leaf Storm and Other Stories*, *Chronicle of a Death Foretold*, *Love in the Time of Cholera*, *The General in His Labyrinth*, and the internationally best-selling *One Hundred Years of Solitude*—he was awarded the Nobel Prize for Literature in 1982. He lives in Mexico City.

A Note on the Type

This book was set on the Linotype in Janson, a recutting made directly from type cast from matrices long thought to have been made by the Dutchman Anton Janson, who was a practicing type founder in Leipzig during the years 1668–87. However, it has been conclusively demonstrated that these types are actually the work of Nicholas Kis (1650–1702), a Hungarian, who most probably learned his trade from the master Dutch type founder Dirk Voskens. The type is an excellent example of the influential and sturdy Dutch types that prevailed in England up to the time William Caslon developed his own incomparable designs from them.

Composed by Heritage Printers, Inc.,
Charlotte, North Carolina
Printed and bound by R. R. Donnelley & Sons,
Harrisonburg, Virginia
Typography and binding design by
Dorothy S. Baker